BLOW AWAY

BLOW AWAY

Nowhere USA Book Six

NINIE HAMMON

STERLING & STONE

Chapter One

*N*EB *T*ACKETT *PICKS up the shot glass off the bar and knocks the drink back in one swallow, wipes his mouth with the back of his hand. Lifting his boot down off the bar rail, Neb ...*

No, not Neb. Something else, something sexier. Tex. No, Tack! Short for Tackett. Yeah. Folks call him Tack.

*T*ACK *FEELS the liquid warm him throat to groin, though his groin don't need no booze for that. Thinking 'bout dropping a man with one shot turns him on like bedding a good woman. Tack sets the shot glass down on the bar with a clunk and casts a glance at the bartender. Whiskey Joe is slowly drying a glass — well, shining it 'cause it's already dry — and their eyes meet. Tack nods, barely dips his chin ...*

*T*ACK'S *C*HIN has a dent in it, one of them cleft things like Kirk Douglas. And he needs a shave, too, has a day's growth of beard on his face.

. . .

TACK TURNS his back on Whiskey Joe and strides across the room that smells like beer and worn leather and old sweat, his spurs making a clinking sound with every step.

Lily rushes to him, puts her hand on his arm, gently holding him back.

"Tack ... please." Her voice is deep and throaty.

No, not a deep voice. A high voice — but not squeaky. Tinkle-y. Like wind chimes, sorta.

"DON'T DO IT," Lily begs and her voice sounds like little bells ringing.

Tack looks down into her big brown eyes as they fill with tears.

"It's my job, Lily. You know that. Now step aside."

"But they say the El Dorado Kid is lightning fast."

Tack smiles that crooked grin of his that melts women's hearts, reaches out and brushes a strand of Lily's long red hair back from her face.

No, blonde hair, like May Ella Martin's who'd lived at the bottom of the hill — the Martins who had a phone and people left messages there for the Tacketts. Him and May Ella had sex in the old chicken house behind her daddy's barn but didn't nobody know and then she dumped him. But Lily's beautiful, ain't dish-faced like May Ella Martin. Lily looks like ... like ... *Elizabeth Taylor!* Yeah, and Lily has black hair, too, just like Elizabeth Taylor's and her eyes is *violet* like that.

. . .

TACK LOOKS down into Lily's violet eyes and says, "Then I guess I'll have to be faster than lightning."

She bows her head and her shoulders shake but she doesn't cry out loud because everybody knows Tack likes his women strong.

"This won't take long." He brushes past her.

"I love you," she says.

No, she doesn't say it out loud. She whispers it, doesn't mean for him to hear it but he does.

I LOVE YOU, too, Tack thinks but doesn't say it out loud because Tack can't love any woman. He lives every day on the razor's edge of danger … it wouldn't be fair to ask a woman to share a life like that.

Pushing through the swinging doors, he steps out onto the wooden sidewalk and a little freckle-faced kid runs up to him.

"Gee, sheriff, can I see your guns?"

"Why sure you can, son."

In a movement that's too fast to follow, Tack crosses his arms in front and snatches the Colt .45 from his left holster with his right hand, and the one in his right holster—

"WHATCHA DOING, NEB?"

Zach was standing on the top step of the porch that wrapped around the back of the house. It was screened-in so's you could sit out there at night and not get eat alive by mosquitoes. Neb fumbled and dropped one gun into the grass, hadn't even been able to get the pistol on his right hip out of the holster at all.

"Ain't none of your business what I'm doin'!"

Neb didn't even look at Zach. Nebuchadnezzar Tackett was Viola's oldest son and that meant he had ought to be respected by his younger brothers. They'd ought to listen to him and do what he told them. Well, all except Malachi and he didn't do what anybody told him — not even Mama.

Kneeling in the grass, Neb picked up the shiny Colt .45 pistol that him, Obie and Zach had took when they broke into Lester Peetree's hardware store last week. They stole pro'lly two dozen firearms, all kinds and sizes. Took every shell of ammunition they could find, too. Neb wasn't rightly sure why it was Mama'd wanted all that, then figured out she didn't want it — she just didn't want nobody else to have it. Zach'd said he thought Mama intended to gather up all the guns in the whole county eventually, and maybe she did. Neb hoped so 'cause then she wouldn't never notice that he'd snatched the matching pair of .45 pistols with the pearl-handled grips and their soft leather holsters from the haul at Peetree's, never even showed 'em to her, kept them pistols for his own.

"Mama called from the courthouse and said for you and me to go back out to Howie Witherspoon's place and see did him and the kid come back yet."

They'd gone out the day before, beat on the door, looked all around but couldn't find him — which didn't make no sense 'cause his car was in the driveway.

"You and Obie go. I'll stay here with Essie."

Esther Ruth didn't never need nobody to stay home and babysit her until they moved out of the house in Turkey Neck Hollow and into this big place on Main Street in Persimmon Ridge. She usta stay at home all day by herself and she'd be fine, just sit in the sunshine rocking back and forth, singing her song. They'd only been here two days, though, since Mama kicked old man Nower out on Sunday, and Essie hadn't got used to it yet, was scared to be here alone.

"Mama said for you and me to go. She told Obie to stay here and mow the grass."

Mow the grass. Good luck with that! It was six inches tall and so thick it gummed up the mower blades. Neb had mowed part of the backyard 'fore he give up and he had to stop every twenty feet or so to clean the clumps of wet grass out of the blades. If it wasn't mow the grass, it was trim the rose bushes. They had thorns, would scratch your hands like you'd got hold of a bobcat. Sweep the porches. They hadn't had no yard or flowers on Gizzard Ridge and if anybody'd ever swept the porch there, Neb hadn't seen 'em do it. But there was always some kinda job to do around the Nower House — *the Tackett House*. It'd took him and Zach half the afternoon yesterday to dig up that National Historic Landmark sign out of the front yard. If Mama heard Neb call it the Nower House, she'd skin him alive.

Getting to his feet, Neb fit the pistol back into the holster on his belt and when he did he seen what the problem was. You could draw both guns at the same time straight out, but if you wanted to do a cross-handed draw, you had to turn the holsters around backward on the belt. Them holsters wasn't made to pull the guns out from the front side.

Now that he'd figured it out, he'd get it right. Just needed to practice, that's all. He'd work on it again soon's he got back.

"Won't take no time at all to get there in *my* car," Zach said, his chest all puffed out. He'd stole Bud Griffith's black Corvette and woulda drove it around all day long if Mama hadn't told him he was too old for such foolishness. Neb'd thought about picking hisself out a car but didn't see no point in it since all the gas was gonna run out eventually. But Mama wasn't worried about that a'tall, had some plan in mind she hadn't told nobody about. Mama always had a plan.

"That 'Vette's only got seats for two people." Neb crossed the yard to the porch. "So where was it you's plannin' on puttin' the Witherspoon guy and his kid when we find 'em?" Neb sneered. "Maybe we could tie a rope to their feet and drag 'em."

Zach was itching to drive that car so bad he hadn't thought about that part. Neb shook his head. His younger brother couldn't be trusted to put his pants on with the fly in the font, wouldn't surprise Neb to see him walking around with the zipper up his butt.

"We'll use Obie's Ford." Obie had come home last night with a black Ford pickup. Stole it from somebody but Neb didn't know who. "Put the both of 'em in the back like bales of hay. You get the keys while I put these away." Neb kept the guns out of sight 'cause Mama might see 'em and fancy 'em and take 'em away from him.

The phone rang inside. Mama. When it was him and his brothers in the sheriff's office at the courthouse — throwing darts or playing cards — and Mama was home, she'd call about every five minutes wanting something. Neb thought Mama liked having a phone right there in her own house so she made up excuses to use it. Of course, he had better sense than to say a thing like that to Mama. He wasn't stupid!

He heard Obie talking in the den when he went upstairs to put the gun and gun belt under his bed — in a bedroom he didn't have to share with nobody! Apparently, Mama wanted to know if him and Zach had left yet.

"They been gone about ten minutes, Mama," he heard Obie lie, then pause. "Yes, ma'am, I's on my way out to crank up the mower when the phone rang."

Soon's Obie hung up, Zach looked up at Neb coming down the stairs. "Obie won't give me the keys."

"I don't like other people drivin' my truck," Obie whined at Neb.

"*Yore* truck? How you figure being selfish with a truck that don't even b'long to you?"

"Does, too. I took it and now it's mine. Same's Zach's car. Mama said for you and *Zach* to go find Howie so you can take Zach's car."

Neb sighed. The two of them sounded like little kids fighting in a sandbox. Neb started to lay down the law, but didn't bother. They wasn't gonna need Obie's truck to haul Howie and his brat back into town because they wasn't gonna find them. They'd searched the Witherspoon place top to bottom yesterday when Mama sent them looking the first time. Howie Witherspoon was long gone.

"C'mon, then," he told Zach. "I got things to do."

Soon's him and Zach was done with their wild goose chase out to the Witherspoon place, Neb'd come back home and practice, would turn them holsters around backward so's the pistols would slide out fast.

Fast as lightning.

No, *faster* than lightning.

Chapter Two

CHARLIE SHOT MALACHI a look over Sam's head and he nodded. The look said: I'm worried about Sam. And Sam did look terrible — well, as terrible as it was possible to look with a china-doll face and glossy red hair. As Malachi studied her profile now, with her attention focused on the little boy lying on the bed, he was reminded what a beautiful woman she was.

But right now that beautiful woman was worn out, had exhaustion — both physical and emotional — stamped on her face. Malachi was certain she had not slept a wink, had sat up in the chair beside Rusty's bed, vigilant. Hoping, praying he would wake up. But he had not.

He glanced at Rusty, his face so still, his features outlined in the glow of the lamp on the table beside the bed. It wasn't a hospital-room lamp. Malachi had brought it down from E.J.'s apartment upstairs because the lone pull-chain light in the middle of the ceiling in the converted stockroom provided little light and the illumination was harsh and garish, like a police lineup. The lamplight was softer, cast a warm glow on the side of the boy's face. He seemed much younger than twelve, like a little boy fast asleep, a handsome kid, looked like his mother.

"I won't bother to try to get you to take a break," Charlie told Sam. "I know you won't. But I *can* make toast, though it's the outside limit of my culinary skill. I made some in E.J.'s toaster upstairs. Two heels, the last of the loaf and the bread's stale — but you won't taste it anyway. I brought a jar of Mama's fruit preserves from home just to entice you." Charlie held out a plate to Sam. "Just a couple of bites."

Sam gave Charlie a wan smile. "I appreciate the effort but I'm not—"

"Would you take that as an answer?" Malachi said firmly. "If you had a patient who clearly needed some food in her stomach — to keep her strength up — would you let them off the hook because they weren't hungry?" He held up his hand before she could protest more. "It is humanly possible to consume food even if you're not hungry. Just ask any Marine grunt. At the end of a fifteen-mile hike with full pack, you think you're too tired to eat, but if you don't, the sergeant will stand on your chest and force the food down your throat."

She still hesitated.

"You *reeeeally* don't want me to stand on your chest and force this toast down your throat."

She reached out and picked up a piece. Charlie'd slathered it in strawberry preserves. When she took only a small bite, Malachi scowled at her and she swallowed and took another bite, a normal one.

"The jam's good," she told Charlie in a voice that sounded as thin and dry as autumn leaves scraping across a sidewalk.

Rusty lay on his right side, perfectly still beneath the white sheet. Sam had wrapped the bandages she'd put on his back all the way around his chest, so he was encased in white gauze from his shoulders to his waist. They'd carried the boy into the building from the parking lot after crazy Claire McFarland had forced him to "ride the Jabberwock" with the dead body of her son — for reasons that made sense only in her twisted mind.

When they'd placed Rusty on his belly on the long metal-tray exam table and Malachi got a good look at his back, an unexpected wave of pure rage had washed over him. Claire McFarland had *shot* the kid! Shot him in the back with a shotgun loaded with buckshot. Malachi had coldcocked her in the parking lot and confiscated the shotgun, but when he'd seen Rusty's back, he'd wanted to go back out to the parking lot and hit her again. Might even have done it but Raylynn said her husband had shown up and taken her home. And Lester Peetree — dependable Lester Peetree — had taken Douglas's body back to Bascum's Funeral Home.

While Sam and Charlie had carefully picked pieces of buckshot out of the flayed skin on the boy's back, Malachi had gone to Martha Whittiker's house looking to "borrow" a bed. Martha now lay with her grandson in side-by-side body drawers in the basement of Bascum's, so she wouldn't miss it. Malachi had found a single bed with a metal frame in her spare bedroom and brought it back to the clinic to set up in the storage room Sam had turned into a hospital room for Rusty. Just down the hall in the veterinary clinic, E.J. lay in a real hospital bed. Roscoe Tungate's late wife had ALS and he'd gotten a hospital bed and moved it into his living room so he and his daughters could care for her at home until she died. After E.J. was mauled by Judd Perkins's rabid dog, Roscoe had hauled the bed to the veterinary clinic in the Middle of Nowhere. But if there was another hospital bed floating around somewhere in the county, Malachi didn't know where.

Sam had bandaged Rusty and started an IV to replace the fluids oozing out of the weeping wound on his back. She was careful to move him as little as possible because the wound you could see was not nearly as threatening and terrifying as the one you couldn't see. Blood had been seeping out of his ear and he was unconscious. They all vividly remembered what the repeat ride on the Jabberwock had done to Abby Clayton. A stroke and brain damage. And her third ride had …

Rusty still had not regained consciousness. Malachi was certain every minute that boy lay on the bed unresponsive, his mother was dying a thousand lifetimes. Sam was a good mother. Rusty was lucky to have her. And the boy was a good kid, a real good kid. If anything happened to him …

Like Sam had said yesterday, kneeling on the asphalt beside the unconscious boy, "We have to get out of here."

Lives hung in the balance — E.J.'s, Grace Tibbits's, Pete Rutherford's, and now Rusty's. All four of them needed medical care they couldn't get here. Not to mention the lives of every man, woman and child in Nowhere County, as the Jabberwock prowled the countryside, "absorbing" one after the other of them. It would keep taking people until there was nobody left if they couldn't figure out what it was and how to beat it.

They'd been discussing that very thing with Thelma Jackson yesterday when the latest crisis exploded like a mortar shell all around them. First, Skeeter Burkett had brought in a body he'd found in the river downstream from the Scott's Ridge Overlook. And then Rusty had shown up in the parking lot after his first Jabberwock ride, bringing his friend Douglas Taylor to get medical help because Douglas had been bitten by a rattlesnake.

All that followed those two bombshells had left them too frazzled and distracted to concentrate. Now, they had to regain their focus to solve the Jabberwock puzzle. A clock was ticking, counting relentlessly down to death for everybody in the county.

Sam finished one piece of toast and resolutely refused the second, waving it off with a dismissive "Later." She reached over and took her little boy's limp hand, squeezed it and turned to the others.

"Drag some chairs in here and sit down. I'm not leaving Rusty, but we have to talk! I've been doing nothing but thinking about the Jabberwock for the past … whatever, all night … and I got nothing. I am no closer to figuring this thing out than we were when Thelma left yesterday afternoon."

She looked earnestly from one to the other. "I'm too fried. You guys are going to have to …"

"There still are things we don't know and haven't done yet," Charlie said and Sam nodded.

"We need to go back to Charlie's mother's house and see if we can get … see if we can talk to the Jabberwock somehow through the chalkboard." The chalkboard had contained a cryptic message from the beast on Saturday. Charlie'd written "I want to go home" and the monster had responded, "No, stay here and play with me." They'd intended to go back to her house to see if they could use the blackboard to crank up a conversation with the beast, but then Skeeter had brought in Hayley Norman's mangled corpse and …

"We need to have a chat with Fish, too, find out why he blurted out the word Jabberwock after we'd all ridden it for the first time two weeks ago," said Malachi. "How'd he know the thing's name, and what else does he know about it that he's not telling?"

"All that stuff Thelma left," Sam said. "It's still in the breakroom. Notes on what that old woman, the witch's daughter, told her. That list of names from the Bible. I guess we need to go through it all and ... I don't know what."

"I'll take it home with me. Maybe after Merrie goes to sleep tonight, I can take a look at it. Right now, though, we have to ..." Charlie didn't finish. Said merely, "Liam."

Liam had been shot and killed on Saturday, murdered in front of hundreds of witnesses, none of whom would admit to seeing a thing. Today was Tuesday. His body, along with the bodies of a growing number of dead — mostly murdered — people was in one of the refrigerated drawers in the basement of Bascum's funeral home.

"I've been working on that," Malachi said. "I talked to a couple of guys who're willing to dig a grave in the Ridge cemetery." Located on the outskirts of Persimmon Ridge, the cemetery's name was inscribed in wrought-iron letters on the archway across the entrance: Cherry Blossom Acres. Nobody'd ever called it that. "I'd a whole lot rather have a casket, even a wooden coffin, but ..." Malachi paused. "If I were going to ask anybody to build a coffin, it would have been Reece Tibbits in that woodshed of his. But nobody's seen him in a couple of days. And his house has ..."

"Aged?" Sam's voice was barely a whisper. The horror of that still had the power to knock the wind out of them.

"We will just have to use a plastic body bag. We can lay our hands on those. There are several floating around — at the fire department, the sheriff's office, Bascum's. We could get a grave ready and then ..."

"Yeah, then what? We can't just ..." Charlie didn't finish.

"No, we won't. We'll have … something, some kind of service," Sam said.

"Reverend Norman won't be officiating," Charlie said, and she turned to Malachi. "My car's parked out front. Mama's car." She reached into the pocket of her jeans, fished out a set of car keys and handed them to him. "You told Rev. Norman you'd pick him up at nine, right?"

Malachi had, indeed, promised to take the minister out to Scott's Ridge Overlook, where the minister's murdered daughter had left the family's lone remaining car.

"Didn't that strike you as … weird?" Charlie said. "The way he asked you to take him out to retrieve his car. I mean — why *you*?"

"He *said* he didn't want to break down in front of somebody from his congregation," Malachi said.

"And you bought that explanation?" Charlie asked.

"Nope. That's not the real reason, but what is?" Malachi couldn't figure it out, just knew he had a "bad feeling about this, Luke" sense about the whole thing. "I'm supposed to pick him up in a few minutes. I'll come back here when I'm finished and we can figure out … Liam. And maybe take a shot at communicating through that blackboard."

"While *you're* running your taxi service" — Charlie looked at Sam — "how about *I* borrow Sam's car and see if I can track down Fish?"

"You sure you want to do that?" Sam asked. "Shouldn't you stay out of sight?"

"No … I don't think that's a good idea. "

Malachi heard both fear and resolve in Charlie's voice. He'd seen it played out time and time again — a crisis brought out the best in good people and the worst in bad. The two girls he'd played with as children had both grown up to be strong women, tough. He was proud of them. But his mother had proved to be even more vicious than he'd ever have dreamed. She had threatened to kill Charlie if Malachi bailed on the bargain he'd made with her — and he'd definitely bailed. As soon as his mother figured that out …

"It seems to me that the best place to hide is in plain sight," Charlie said. "We're running a bluff here and I think it looks less suspicious if I just … go on about life."

Charlie would be in real danger if his mother found out Malachi had defied her — that'd he'd killed Howie Witherspoon against her express hands-off orders. But Malachi was sure his mother didn't know that yet, probably hadn't even missed Howie and certainly didn't know what'd happened to him. Malachi'd dumped his body in an abandoned mine shaft. Might be nobody would ever find it.

"Maybe you're right. Mama will leave Charlie alone as long as I toe the line and as far as she knows, I'm still 'toe-ing.'" He paused. "And we need all hands on deck."

The door to the room suddenly burst open and Merrie came barreling in, "Mommy, Mommy, you gotta come see dis." She grabbed Charlie's hand and started dragging her to the door. "Come look. Da puppies-es eyes are open. Dey waking up."

Malachi saw Sam's attention snap back to her son, lying so still on the bed — Rusty, who was *not* waking up.

"You guys go do what you have to do and I'll be here … with Rusty." Sam had to struggle now to control her emotions.

Malachi stood, leaned over and put his hand on Sam's shoulder. "We'll figure this out. We will. We'll get Rusty out of here."

She smiled up at him, clearly not convinced. But that was okay because he wasn't either.

Chapter Three

JOLENE RUTHERFORD SAT PROPPED up on the army surplus store cot on the pillows Cotton Jackson had brought back with him from Danville. She suspected it was long past dawn out there on the flat, remembering a childhood lived in the shadow of mountains so tall the sun didn't clear the peaks until ten in the morning. Her pain level was tolerable now, not because of the pillows but because of what else Cotton had brought back along with them.

Oxycontin, which she'd heard was as easy to get in eastern Kentucky as popcorn at a carnival and apparently she'd heard right. Cotton would only say, "I know a guy who knows a guy," pointing out that even with mandatory drug testing, the foreman of a factory had to be on the lookout for shift workers who might be using. He'd only had to make a couple of calls, found what he was looking for near the little town of Simpsonville in Drayton County, and then went on into Danville to pick up sterile bandages and surgical tape for Jolene's wound.

She could hear the rumble of low voices from the kitchen, where Stuart McClintock and Cotton had gone so she could "get some rest." They hadn't said, "sleep," because nobody in Cotton's almost-empty house had looked forward to nodding off last night — and greeting the nightmares they'd been sure awaited them.

Staying awake was better. Not easier — particularly in view of all the sleep they'd lost since they got here — but it was definitely better. She probably could have made out what Stuart and Cotton were saying if she concentrated. But she was feeling just enough of a fuzzy buzz to be unwilling to make the effort. Besides, they were obviously talking about their little adventure with the monsters in Fearsome Hollow late yesterday afternoon — both human and otherwise, and she was worn out with that subject.

Somebody had shot at them. With a high-powered deer rifle — Cotton was a hunter and he knew the sound, said the damage to her van was consistent with the firepower of such a weapon. Bottom line, somebody'd been trying to kill them.

Jolene burped out something like a laugh and felt her bandaged arm protest.

"Oops, sorry 'bout that," she told her arm, and realized that she might be higher than she'd thought. Not being a recreational drug user like most everybody in her world, she didn't know how taking a heavy-duty narcotic was supposed to make you feel. It was indeed a pleasant sensation, she'd grant that, but her quarrelsome bullet wound kept her from floating out into la-la land.

Bullet wound.

She'd been shot.

Shot.

Okay, maybe she wasn't as worn out with the subject as she thought, since it kept hitting her in waves of realization like breakers on a rocky beach. With the edges of reality softened by the drug, the memories were fragmented, just pieces, each one jagged and sharp.

RAIN. Then no rain. An umbrella of mist above them. Shadows, black holes ripped in the fabric of the universe.

The sound, the cry of someone, something in horrible pain.

She turns the dial, flips a switch and a reverberation all around sounds like a gong inside a bell jar.

Pressure.

She can't breathe.

Her fingers searching, find wires, pull them out and the pressure stops.

The van window explodes, pain slices her arm.

Darkness.

Jolene! Jolene!

Someone's calling her name from a long way off. Her eyes snap open and a black face is peering down at her.

Stuart McClintock.

THEN JOLENE's memories suddenly snapped into focus, like she'd been taking an eye exam and the optometrist asked, "Is this clearer ... or *this*?"

There'd been a mighty roaring sound — that memory was vivid, the rumble of wind blowing in the broken-out windows.

Stuart had lifted Jolene up off the floor and into a sitting position in the back of the van as they careened around corners in their desperate flight away from Gideon and Fearsome Hollow — *where someone had been shooting at them.* He had unceremoniously yanked open her blouse to get a look at the wound in her upper arm just below her shoulder, the flaming brand on her skin, a hot poker.

She turned and looked full at it then. Blood was streaming down her arm to her elbow from a … cut probably three inches long across her arm.

Not a cut!

A bullet wound. Except the bullet hadn't punctured, it had just sliced across the skin. Grazed her, as they'd have said if this had been a cowboy movie.

Stuart poked around on it, then sat back panting, and it was only then she realized he'd been holding his breath.

"Pull over, Cotton," he called out, but Cotton paid him no mind, kept the pedal to the metal, speeding down the winding mountain roads. "I said *pull over.* Before you miss a turn and we fly off the road into … nothing."

Cotton neither slowed down nor pulled over.

"We got to get Jolene to the emergency room!" he said.

"Not at the risk of life and limb we don't. It's not that bad, really."

Stuart looked at her and forced a smile. "I guess that's easy for me to say, but it really doesn't appear to be life-threatening." He cried out to Cotton, "This gunshot wound isn't going to kill her but crashing down a mountainside will. Now, *pull over.*"

Cotton slowed, pulled off on the shoulder of the road and stopped. He turned around in the seat and even from her position on the floor in the back, Jolene could see his hands shaking. Yeah, they were way safer sitting here than they were with him driving.

"You alright — really?" Cotton didn't wait for an answer but asked Stuart. "You're saying she's okay, it's not bad?"

She was suddenly cold — not surprising since she was wet, though not soaked to the skin like Stuart and Cotton. But maybe the shakes were more about the blood running down her arm from a gunshot wound than from her wet clothing.

"Crank the heat," Stuart told Cotton and he did, which would have been more helpful if the wind wasn't blowing rain in through the two windows that had been shot out.

Shot out!

Gunfire.

"Who was *shooting* at us?" she managed to stammer.

"How would *I* know?" Stuart said, as he ripped a piece of fabric off the padding she kept wrapped around her equipment when she traveled.

"Who would want to hurt us?" Cotton asked.

They batted who and why questions around while Stuart put a makeshift bandage on Jolene's arm. She winced every time he touched it, couldn't help it. She was trying as hard as she could to make it seem like the gouged-out wound across her upper arm was no big deal, wanted Stuart and Cotton to think it didn't hurt at all, wanted them to understand that it wasn't serious. And it wasn't, it really wasn't. But it did hurt. No way around that. It did hurt.

When it was finally clear not a one of them had a clue why somebody had been shooting at them, or who "somebody" might be, Cotton shifted the focus.

"We can talk about all this while we drive. We can make the emergency room in twenty minutes." Twenty minutes with jet packs! Then Jolene realized Cotton was talking about going to Crawford Memorial in Morgantown. On the east side of Nowhere County, the Crawford County hospital was closer than the bigger one in Carlisle in Beaufort County to the north.

"So are you volunteering to be the one who explains to the police how I got this?" Jolene asked.

"Police?" Cotton said. "I'm not taking you to the police, I'm taking you to an emergency room."

"Where they will call the police." Stuart said. Clearly, Cotton didn't get it yet. "They'll have to, no choice. I don't know the specifics of the statute in the state of Kentucky, but they're pretty standard in every state. Hospitals are required by law to report all bullet wounds to the police."

"Fine, then, we'll tell the police that we were … that somebody shot at us while …" Cotton ran out of gas.

"Well, you see, it's like this, officer," Jolene said. "We were using a ghost-zapper on the spirits in Gideon — you know the place where everybody vanished in a puff of smoke a hundred years ago — and suddenly somebody started using us for target practice."

"But we have to report—"

"Like you reported all the missing people?" Stuart said. "How'd that work out for you?"

"You saying you think the police would forget—?"

"If they come here to investigate, yeah, they'll forget. As a former recipient of a Jabberwock mind wipe, I am here to testify those officers won't remember a thing!"

So they'd driven to Cotton's house instead of to Morgantown, then he'd gone to Drayton County to get the drugs. He'd brought back bandages, tape, pillows, and more Colonel Poc Poc from Danville, but nobody had an appetite.

And then they talked. And talked. Chased their tails until they all were exhausted. Finally, Jolene begged off and the men made her as comfortable as they could in Cotton's guest bedroom.

Where she'd sat all night, struggling not to nod off even though the drug fuzziness was a lead weight on her eyelids. She knew the meanest monsters in the junkyard lived behind her closed eyes.

Now, at last, it was morning. Somehow, staying awake in the daylight didn't seem like such a Herculean task. As she sat with her arm throbbing while the men talked about monsters and gunshots, she thought about her phone call to Moses Weiss, and the crazy message she'd left him. It was only now that it occurred to her that Moses might, indeed, have returned her phone call — but nobody'd been here yesterday to answer it. And in Cotton Jackson's gutted house, there was no answering machine to record a message.

It was far more likely that Moses had written her off as the lunatic she must have sounded like. If she'd gotten a message like that, she'd have been calling out the dudes in the white coats to haul the caller off to Saint Somebody's Home for the Bewildered.

Still … maybe, *maybe* Moses might help.

Chapter Four

DUNCAN NORMAN STOOD at the front window looking out, waiting for Malachi Tackett to pull into the driveway to pick him up. To give him a ride out to Scott's Ridge so he could get the car Hayley had left there when …

The room behind him was filled with people, church members, come to pay their respects and … and what else? He didn't know.

He felt a hand on his arm and had to fight the urge to cringe away. It was Miriam, his wife of eighteen years, who had a right to expect that her husband would be a comfort to her when she lost her only daughter. He'd vowed to cherish her and take care of her when the two of them stood before Brother Homer Sellers in the Sacred Covenant Holiness Church in Hazard, pledging themselves to each other and their lives to God's service.

Duncan had been so head-over-heels in love — but had kept his passion in check for two years while he finished his seminary training at the College of the Scriptures in Louisville. He had almost wrecked his car in his headlong dash to a motel where they could finally consummate their union.

As he recalled, that first time hadn't gone too well. But Miriam was a good Christian woman and he didn't expect her to enjoy it. Sex was for procreation and from their union had come a child, a single child, a precious little girl — whose broken body now lay in a refrigerated drawer in the basement of Bascum's Funeral Home.

Malachi Tackett had killed her. And he would pay. Duncan would deal out the full measure of retribution.

"Duncan, we need to talk about … the service," Miriam said.

For a moment he didn't know what she was talking about. It was only then that he realized he saw no future of any kind out there before him, couldn't conceive of … of life *after*. He would kill Malachi Tackett and then … nothing. Darkness. A void. He looked down into Miriam's face and tried to connect with her, tried to envision the two of them going on beyond now, here, today. But there was only darkness.

"We'll talk when I get back," he said.

"But … Harvey could go out there and get the car, why do you—?"

"No!" he snapped and saw heads turn his way. "It's something I need to do. By myself. Please understand." She didn't, but he didn't care, just turned back to the window, looking for a car to pull into the driveway.

Duncan hadn't even tried to go to sleep last night, had merely showered and changed clothes at first light. He didn't want to look like a derelict, rumpled and unshaven, because that would give everyone even more ammunition to use to blast through his reserve and get him to take a tranquilizer or "pray with me" or let out his feelings. Or something. They all wanted something from him and didn't realize he had nothing to give them. That he was hollow. That inside his chest was a vast frozen wasteland where a chilly wind blew. He was empty.

Except he wasn't, not as he had been when the news of Hayley's death knocked the breath out of him, knocked his soul out of him. Something had seeped into him since then, slowly, relentlessly filled the void. He couldn't put his finger on what it was. No, didn't *want* to name it. Just thought of it as a "sinister force" that had taken up residence in him. And its presence revealed other things, opened up a whole world he'd always known existed but had never before experienced. Of course, Duncan knew the world was populated by … evil things. Scripture said so and "if Scripture says it, I believe it, and that's the end of it." But now he could *almost* see them. Creatures lurking on the edge of his vision, things you couldn't look at straight up or they'd vanish. Things you didn't want to see straight up. Behind him in the bathroom mirror this morning when he shaved. Beside him now, reflected in the window pane as he looked out. Evil was real. Satan was real. And … *demons* were real, too. He understood that now in a palpable way he never had before.

Duncan had come back from the Middle of Nowhere yesterday and barricaded himself in his office, refusing to see anyone until he could tell by the timber of the voices beyond the door that people were so concerned about him someone was going to intervene soon. He knew it was better to cut them off at the knees. So he'd come out long enough to nod his head up and down or shake it side to side like a good little bobblehead doll to the questions put to him.

Are you okay?

Nod.

Is there anything you need?

Shake.

Do you want to talk about it?

Shake.

Pray about it?

Shake.

Can we get you something to eat?

Shake.

The house smelled like Thanksgiving on steroids. The casserole dishes were stacked three deep on the countertops. Where did all the food come from? Nobody'd been able to go to the grocery store in two weeks — how did they get the ingredients to …?

He let it go. He didn't care. Didn't care about anything.

Correction. He cared about two things. Laying his hands on a gun. And using it to put a hole in Malachi Tackett's chest.

He'd accomplished the first on his way home yesterday from the Middle of Nowhere. He'd known he couldn't ask to borrow a weapon! That would have been tossing a match into a bucket of gasoline. Everyone would have assumed he intended to commit suicide and then he wouldn't have been allowed to be alone even to take a piss.

Then he'd thought about Whitt Gibney.

Whitt was the volunteer custodian of two of the churches whose congregations Duncan served in his circuit of pastor-less churches in Nowhere and surrounding counties. Praying Hands Pentecostal Church in Wiley was the largest, by comparison only, with maybe fifty people on the church rolls, though only a handful ever showed up at one time for services. The Nower Pentecostal Church in Pine Bluff Hollow was the oldest congregation, worshipped in a little church building that had a belfry — but no bell — and a sign out front that teenagers had vandalized. That's where Duncan had gone, knowing Whitt wouldn't be there, of course, it being a Monday.

Whitt was an odd duck. He was short, maybe five feet, two inches … on tiptoes, and had the worst case of Little Man Syndrome Duncan had ever seen. Had a chip on his shoulder the size of Greenland and raging paranoia, which might or might not be drug related. Duncan suspected he was a dealer, was certain he was a user and had endured so many of Whitt's the-gubmint's-comin'-to-get-our-guns rants that he was certain the man's home up in Freeman Hollow was an arsenal. He wasn't sure about that, but what he was sure about was that Whitt kept a pistol on the top shelf above the toilet in the cubby-hole bathroom in the little building on Norton Lane — behind the cleaning supplies. You know, so the gubmint wouldn't catch him unarmed with his pants down.

Duncan didn't know what kind of pistol it was, had discovered it accidentally one rainy Saturday when he'd gone looking for drain cleaner after he'd flushed the toilet and sewage backed up into the baptistry. And there it was on the top shelf, tucked away behind a bottle of Drano.

From the Middle of Nowhere, Duncan had driven Mamie Butterfield's borrowed Pontiac down back roads instead of straight down Danville Pike — Barber's Mill Road to Gallagher Station to Route 15, then Little Knob Road to Norton Lane. He'd prayed the whole way the gun was still there. No! He hadn't *prayed*. He had hoped. Duncan Norman could not pray. A blackness had welled up in his chest and blotted out all of God's light as he read the lurid description in Hayley's diary about being raped by a *tall, dark man with a rugged face, unruly black hair and piercing blue eyes.*

Malachi Tackett. In almost two decades serving nowhere people in churches in Wiley, Twig, Killarney,

Frogtown, Persimmon Ridge and Poorfolk, performing weddings and funerals and christenings, Duncan Norman had seen the faces of everyone who lived here and nobody fit Hayley's description better than Malachi did.

Malachi Tackett — the son of *Viola* Tackett was capable of that kind of monstrous act. Hayley'd known the man who had … She'd trusted him. And he had ravished her!

The gun was still behind the Drano bottle when Duncan felt around on the shelf for it. He didn't know a whole lot about firearms, but knew enough. It wasn't a very big gun, but that was good because he had to hide it — in his suitcoat jacket, his pants pocket, in his belt — somewhere. it was the kind of gun that had a cylinder that spun around. He found the catch, clicked it open, checked to make sure it was loaded. Of course it would be. What good would an empty gun do Whitt when the gubmint showed up to drag him away?

He felt around on the shelf again and found a full box of ammo — a bonus — and he put the extra shells in his pocket.

It'd been almost dark by that time and Duncan knew everybody at his house was frantic because he had been gone so long, but he took the time to go out behind the church building and practice firing the weapon, was glad he had because he hadn't been prepared for how loud it was or that it kicked. Of course, Duncan was no marksman, but he wouldn't have to be. He intended to shoot Malachi Tackett down like a dog, point blank. Without warning. Planned to empty the pistol into his body. Might even reload with the spare shells and fire them, too.

Chapter Five

"HE WASN'T NOWHERE, MA," Zach said.

"We looked and looked," Neb said. "Hollered out 'til we was hoarse."

"You're *sure*?"

They began to protest, told Viola all the places they'd looked, how hard they'd tried and she believed they had. She leaned back in the big chair behind the desk in the sheriff's office and ignored their babbling.

Where had Howie Witherspoon gone? And why? Who runs off without a car? That didn't make no sense. You decided you were gonna boogie, you didn't go on foot — particularly if you're Howie Witherspoon with that bum knee.

And where did he think he could go? The Jabberwock had him locked in same as it did the rest of the county. If he'd tried to escape and showed up in the bus shelter in the Middle of Nowhere puking his guts up, she'd have heard about it. She had eyes everywhere.

And why would he run? He didn't know he needed to. He didn't have no idea she'd decided to use him to solidify her authority. A wife killer — killed a preacher's kid, too. Might be the teenager was pregnant, which made that a whole lot worse. His own little boy — she'd bet dollars to doughnuts he'd offed that kid, too, by now. Soon's he got tanked enough to get up the nerve, he'd have put that kid down.

Three murders. Four if you count the baby that girl was carrying. Why, Viola Tackett would be saving the good citizens of Nowhere County from falling into the clutches of a *serial killer.* Wouldn't be no grumbling about "he didn't do it' when she strung *him* up.

Only he didn't know she'd decided to call in them chips. So why had he run?

"I's thinking 'bout takin' his car," Neb said. "I could hotwire it. The thing's just sitting in his driveway, ain't nobody using it, and I need something to get around in."

Neb wasn't a car nut like Zach, didn't drool over the latest set of shiny wheels. He'd be content with Howie Witherspoon's car, a Dodge something, had that stupid ram's head hood ornament. She'd seen it parked at the Dollar General Store, off to the side to allow paying customers to park in front. Back when there'd been paying customers, before the Middle of Nowhere became the landing zone for Jabberwock victims. They'd about emptied the place out on J-Day, and after that, folks just went in and took whatever they wanted from what little was left. She supposed that was looting, but Howie hadn't been there to stop anybody. Of course, she knew now he'd been busy at the time murdering his wife and burying her body. Some stores in the Ridge, and a couple out in the county were still "open for business," but that'd last only as long as their merchandise held out. Wouldn't be no deliveries to re-stock the shelves. She didn't think they charged "money" now, strictly barter.

"You leave Howie's car right where it's at," she snapped. If she let Neb have the car, she was admitting Howie didn't have no need of it anymore. She didn't like where that kind of thinking took her. But the thought was like a moth battering itself against the window, trying to get in where the light was. Did Malachi have something to do with Howie's disappearance?

She wouldn't let herself give full consideration to the possibility because it was a game-changer if he had. If her son had directly defied her, done something to Howie when she'd expressly told him that Howie was hands-off, that meant … Yeah, what did it mean?

It meant something *ugly* was about to go down and she *pure D* did not want that to happen. Oh, wasn't like she minded making good on her threat to off that Charlie Ryan woman. She looked forward to it — mouthing off like she done in front of other people, disrespecting Viola. Viola'd wanted to smash her like a stinkbug at the time. The woman deserved whatever Viola decided to dish out.

But Malachi. What about *Malachi*?

She could not stop a wave of disappointment from washing over her at the thought. Her baby boy, the only one of her kids worth the gunpowder it'd take to blow him away. Good, strong Malachi. If he'd turned against her …

She didn't think nothin' maudlin as "it'd break her heart." But it would, or would come as close as anything would to breaking Viola Tackett's heart. She had plans for Malachi, had it all mapped out how she was slowly going to bring him back into the fold, to his rightful place among his kin.

If he'd defied her …

Well, she had to find out, had to know one way or the other. She had to figure out what'd happened to Howie Witherspoon and the rest of it would follow.

"You done with us, Mama?" Neb asked. "If you are, Zach can take me back to the Now— back to the house. I got stuff to do."

"What kinda stuff?"

"Just stuff."

"You can walk home from here. Send Obie back to the office when you get there." Viola wanted the sheriff's office manned twenty-four-seven, like a proper law enforcement agency. Betty Greenleaf, the dispatcher, had "volunteered" after the county meeting to stay on, to answer calls. So far, hadn't been no calls, but there remained one functioning police cruiser and Viola intended to make that cruiser hers, was gonna drive around in it, and she wanted to be able to radio in. Like she wanted to use the phone — because she *could*. When Betty didn't show up yesterday, Viola'd sent Obie to her house to drag her in to work. He come back and said ... he said the house was old, roof falling in, wasn't nobody there. Viola's mind bounced right off that and back to Neb. "You finish up the mowing job I bet Obie ain't even started yet."

She turned to Zach. "Zach here's gonna give me a ride in his fancy new car."

"Where we going, Mama?"

"Just a little piece, out to Iron Rock Road. I want to have me a talk with Howie Witherspoon's neighbors, see do any of them know where he run off to."

As they roared out down Main Street, Viola seen Charlie Ryan — McClintock — and her little girl get out of Sam Sheridan's car and head into Peetree's Hardware Store.

Chapter Six

As CHARLIE and Merrie got out of Sam's car in front of the hardware store, a black Corvette barreled down Main Street behind her and she turned to look, but the car was going too fast for her to see who was in it. The day she'd arrived in Nowhere County, a two-week lifetime ago, she'd taken Merrie on a little tour and a black Corvette had blasted past them on Route 15. She'd thought she recognized the driver. Bud Griffith.

Clearly, Bud was not concerned about the shortage of gasoline if he had enough in his tank to go roaring around the Ridge now like some teenager. Maybe he believed all the rumors flying around that Viola Tackett had gasoline — all anybody could ever need. Charlie knew that was just talk, of course. People acted like that woman could do anything!

Before she left the clinic, Charlie had stopped by to check on E.J. Raylynn was sitting with him, and he looked worse than he had yesterday. Every day he looked worse and worse ... She'd asked him if he knew where she might find Fish. Since Holmes Fischer was the county's token homeless person, he might be hard to locate. E.J.'d been too doped up on oxy to be much help, but Raylynn said she'd seen him out back of Peetree's Hardware Store — Lester'd given him a sleeping bag. In the clinic parking lot, she'd run into Pete Rutherford and asked him the same question. He'd told her to try the courthouse.

"All the offices on the first floor's empty — warm in the wintertime because the sheriff's department is in the basement and they keep the heat turned on. Fish has made hisself a little nest sorta in the one that used to be the Property Valuation Administrator's office. If he's not there, I'd try the basement of the Methodist church."

When Lester Peetree told Charlie he hadn't seen Fish, she took Merrie's hand and they walked down the street to the courthouse. As she climbed the steps of the building, Charlie allowed the child's babbling chatter to fill her mind, shoving aside her memories of the last time she'd been in this building, in the upstairs courtroom on Sunday when Viola Tackett had sentenced an innocent teenager to die.

Charlie's running shoes were quiet on the marble floor of the big hallway, but Merrie's hard-soled sandals made little clicking sounds like a tap dancer and the sounds echoed in the cavernous space. So did Merrie's voice.

"… an there's one with a black spot on the top of his head and he bited me."

"Bit you?"

"Uh huh, but it didn't hurt 'cause his teefs is so liddle. He's the one I want. Pleeeeeease, Mommy."

Merrie had been pleading for a puppy ever since she staged a coup at the clinic on J-Day and established her sovereign reign over all the animals, great and small. Charlie suspected if she relented and said yes, the decision would send Merrie into a tailspin because every day she wanted a different puppy.

"I thought you liked the solid black one, the one with white paws."

"I do! I do! But Spot's eyes are still closed an' Tinkerbell's eyes are blue. Well, Raylynn said they might be blue someday."

"Spot ... Tinkerbell ... have you *named*—?"

Merrie reeled off a list of names. One was Light Bulb, another was Poopy — Charlie didn't bother to point out the inappropriateness of that name — and another was Twinkle-Sparkle.

"I named the kitties, too!" She started off down that list of names as they came to the door with Property Valuation Administrator in black letters on the opaque glass window. Charlie supposed she should knock. She did, and called out his name.

"Fish! You home?"

Okay, not "home."

"Are you *here*?"

There was no reply so she knocked and called again, then tried the knob — of course the door was unlocked — and poked her head inside the room. It was bare, all the office furniture long gone, and she could see a pile of what looked like blankets in a far corner by the heat register, a thermos ... and a lone shoe, no mate in sight. A lidless cough syrup bottle lay on its side by the shoe. But no Fish.

She decided to go downstairs to the sheriff's office and ask the dispatcher, Betty Greenleaf, if she'd seen Fish.

Betty wasn't there.

Obediah Tackett was. He was seated in the big chair in the sheriff's office, leaned back with his feet on the desk, smoking a cigar.

Obie was a big man, not as tall as Malachi but at least

six feet, and not as overweight as Neb, but at least thirty or forty pounds over optimum. He carried it well, better than Neb. His shoulders were enormous, and he had a barrel chest and a beer gut that hung out over his belt.

She had never spent much time around any of the Tacketts except Malachi, and whenever she saw one of them, she was struck by the family resemblance, and surprised at how much difference subtle variations among them made.

Their facial features were similar, but Malachi's face was defined by a wide forehead, high cheekbones and an aristocratic nose. The other boys' features were blunt, like clay approximations of the original.

They all had a shock of black hair — except for Neb, who'd gone prematurely bald. All were big, imposing men.

But only Malachi had light eyes — bright blue, sharp and intelligent. His brothers' eyes were dark, muddy brown, almost seemed to mirror their foggy minds. There was no spark in them. Malachi's body was chiseled by years in the military. The others' shapes mirrored their lifestyles — flabby and lazy. Whenever she saw one of his brothers, it was like the man was some shadowy troll, a crude distortion of the Malachi who presented such a presence to the world.

Obie didn't take his feet off the desk and didn't smile when he saw her, was sharp enough to pick up his mother's dislike for Charlie. He scowled, furrowed his brow and barked, "What do you want?"

Charlie didn't think it was a good idea to tell him what she'd really come for, but she refused to be cowed by his rudeness.

"I'm looking for Betty Greenleaf."

"She ain't here, didn't come in. I went out to find her

and wasn't nothing left of her house but a falling-down shack, looked like it was—"

"A hundred years old," she finished for him. "Yeah, I know. There's a lot of that going around these days."

"Huh?"

"Never mind. Sorry to have bothered you."

"Ain't no bother." He picked up the piece of paper that'd been in his hand when she entered. "Ain't doin' nothing." He folded it over once, and sent it sailing across the room. At least that was the intent, but the man couldn't even make a proper paper airplane and it nosedived into the floor in front of Merrie — who, of course, squealed with delight.

"You made da paper fly!" she cried. She picked up the airplane. "I do it!" She threw it but had no more success than Obie'd had.

"You can't just throw it," Obie said, in a much kinder, gentler voice than he'd used for Charlie and she remembered his sister was a forever-little-girl. "You got to hold it right." He set the chair back down on four legs like he might be about to show her what he meant. Charlie took Merrie's hand firmly in hers. She did not have time for a paper-airplane lesson.

"We have to go now. Tell the," Charlie swallowed, "nice man goodbye." Then she dragged the protesting child from the room.

She had better luck at the Methodist church. She could see from the street that the basement door, down a short flight of concrete steps on the side of the building, was standing open. Hopefully, that meant Fish was in residence. As she and Merrie walked across the overgrown, weedy lawn toward the steps she could hear sounds from inside, though she couldn't make out what they were.

Goody, she thought as she drew near — Fish is here and he's drunk.

But Fish wasn't drunk. He was something approaching cold sober. And the sound he was making had nothing to do with music.

Chapter Seven

NEB LEFT the courthouse and walked down the street toward the Nower House — *the Tackett House*. No, it was still the Nower House whether his mama liked it or not. Folks had been calling it that for more than a hundred years and her kicking Sebastian Nower out and stealing it from him might have made it the house where the Tackett family lived but it didn't change what it was, the name of what it was. Whoever had built it got to name it, and that was its name from then on. Folks who come along later didn't get to change that.

Of course, he wouldn't say nothing like that to Mama! She'd have a conniption fit if him or his brothers was to say such a thing.

But it was still true. Just 'cause you couldn't say the truth of a thing didn't make it not so.

Neb crossed the street to the other side 'cause they was more trees over there and he wanted to walk in the shade. He'd heard Zach say he thought they was something funny about the weather, had been since J-Day. Neb'd called him stupid for saying a dumb thing like that but maybe he had been right after all. It wasn't hot in the middle of the day like it was supposed to be, didn't just keep getting hotter all afternoon like it done every other summer in Neb's memory. Midafternoon was s'posed to be "the heat of the day." Neb knew that 'cause his whole life he had avoided doing any more'n he absolutely had to during the heat of the day. Now the whole day passed and there wasn't no such thing.

Neb didn't like to get hot because he sweat when he was hot and his clothes stuck to him and that made him uncomfortable. So that Jabberwock thing was a good one. But the things Neb most didn't like in life the Jabberwock hadn't fixed. He didn't like his mama telling him what to do, bossing him around all the time like he was a little kid. He didn't like Malachi … just flat out didn't like him. Period. Malachi didn't do what Mama said and she didn't do nothing about it and it wasn't fair for Neb to get bossed around and Malachi not.

Neb trudged along down the street, getting more out of sorts the farther he went. He didn't like to walk because the insides of his thighs rubbed together and they'd get raw if he kept at it. He didn't like to do nothing physical because he was big — he wasn't fat or nothing like that! He was just big, that's all, and men was s'posed to be big. But being big made it hard for him to do heavy work and he done whatever he could to get out of it, made his younger brothers do it 'cause they wasn't big like he was.

Even though it wasn't hot, Neb started to sweat, walking along the street toward the Nower House. He liked calling it that in his head because Mama wouldn't like that, and he was madder than usual at Mama today 'cause she'd said he couldn't take Howie Witherspoon's car. Wasn't nothing right or fair about that. Zach took the car he wanted. Obie got that black pickup truck from somewhere. Neb'd ought to be 'lowed pick out a car for himself to drive around.

But Mama said he couldn't have it.

Said Howie'd need it when he come back, which Neb was sure he never would.

One of these days Neb was going to show Mama! He was gonna tell her to leave him alone, that he was a man growed and he didn't need his mama to tell him what to do. He thought about that day a lot, how he'd stand her down and his brothers would be surprised, and proper respectful of him, and all the girls around would get in line to spread their legs for him as the rightful Man of the Tackett Family.

As he walked the final half block up the sidewalk to the Nower House, set back from the street all impressive like it was, he thought about the shiny Colt .45 pistols he hid away in his room. Soon's he sent Obie off to the court-house, he'd get them guns out, turn them holsters around on the belt so's he could draw cross-handed and practice some more. Wouldn't be long 'fore he was the fastest draw in town.

Then, he'd stand up to Mama. Yes, sir. He'd put her in her place then.

And he'd make folks call him Tack instead of Neb. He hated the name Neb. Hated the whole of it worse, wouldn't never even say the whole thing out loud, wouldn't think it even, remembered in embarrassed shame how the kids teased him when he couldn't spell it. Well, he could spell Tack. T.A.C.K. Might even change his last name, too. Yeah, then it'd be all his. It'd be … *Stallion.* He could spell that: S.T.A.L.I.A.N. Or O.N. One or the other. He'd ask Zach and memorize the spelling before he told people that's what they's supposed to call him from now on. Tack Stallion.

He smiled at the thought, actually picked up his pace, hurrying up the sidewalk to the house so's he could send Obie to the courthouse and he could practice quick-draw with his new guns.

Chapter Eight

FISH WAS SCREAMING. Wailing. Shrieking at the top of his lungs, so loud he was clearly in danger of shredding his vocal chords and blowing the top off his head. Except he wasn't making a sound, not a sound anybody could hear. But Fish could hear it. He could hear it and the sound was eviscerating, was ripping his soul to tatters, and then the stripped pieces of it would blow in the hot wind streaming through the hollow part of his chest.

Except his chest wasn't really hollow, not physiologically hollow. Metaphorically hollow, though. Absolutely. Categorically hollow — empty, vacant, a desolate shell that once had housed who he was and now housed the absence of who he was. Because Fish was gone. He had left the building. Holmes Malloy Fischer III was no longer in residence. Stamp all mail *return to sender*. No forwarding address.

He realized he was banging his head against the concrete block he was leaning back against and was grateful that it hurt. He wasn't numb anymore, at least. Not physically numb. But his emotional numbness was wearing off as well and that was not a good thing, absolutely not a good thing.

He opened one eye, looked around, closed it.

Position established. He was sitting on the floor in the corner of the Methodist Church basement, where he had retreated on Sunday night after … after …

He'd been here ever since, had ridden the DTs bucking bronco, not the same wild horse as the Jabberwock, but close. Horrifyingly close. But it was form over substance. The DTs bronco was imaginary, illusory, ephemeral. The Jabberwock horse was real.

What exactly had transpired on Sunday afternoon was a blur, would likely remain so forever, but the vague outlines of it were good enough.

He had watched that poor druggie teenager get railroaded. Watched Viola Tackett sit up there in that judge's seat proclaiming herself the visage of law and order, had hauled that kid in to stand before her and had passed judgement on him.

For killing his grandmother, Martha Whittiker.

Problem: Dylan Shaw didn't kill Martha Whittiker. Fish did. Hadn't meant to. It was an accident. It was, wasn't it? He had been stealing her booze because he had run out, was in her house, in her kitchen and when she came home and grabbed the bottle …

Blank.

Vacant.

Empty spot.

He thought they struggled and she fell to the floor and hit her head. But maybe he'd hit her accidentally with the bottle. One or the other had happened. Must have happened because he wouldn't hurt … would never have … would never …

But she was lying there on her kitchen floor dead, with

blood spreading all around when he came back to himself, so it didn't take a Rhodes Scholar to figure out what'd happened.

He had run. But then, he'd felt guilty. He had returned to make sure she was alright, surely she was alright and he was going to give her the booze he'd stolen and throw himself on her mercy and plead with her to forgive him for being a thief.

But, of course, she wasn't alright. She was dead. So he had done the only thing he could think to do. He had dumped her body in her druggie grandson's garage apartment — only because he thought the kid would get off! Never did he … never would he … Fish had never intended the kid to get in trouble. He was a druggie, a teenager. Nobody in their right mind would hold him responsible for the death of his elderly grandmother. That's what Fish had figured — wrongly, as it turned out. As everything had turned out for Fish — wrong. Fish thought that by the time the Jabberwock dissipated, or left or blew away or whatever it did and the county was back in the real world of real things — then the police would be called but there'd be no evidence by then and they couldn't convict the kid with no evidence and even if they did convict him, they wouldn't do anything with him but sock him away in St. Somebody's Home for the Bewildered Drug Rehab facility until he turned eighteen and that would be a *good* thing. The kid needed to get clean and that would force him to. So really, if you looked at it that way, Fish had done him a favor.

Only he hadn't gotten away with it — the kid hadn't. Fish got away with it but then Viola Tackett set herself up as the grand poobah of law, order, authority, apple pie and the American way and the next thing Fish knew she's scheduled a kangaroo trial for the kid.

And she'd found him guilty.

And she had sentenced him to death. Death by hanging. Right then and there!

Fish couldn't hold still for that, of course. He had let it go on far too long and he couldn't allow the kid to get in trouble for a crime he didn't commit. So Fish had grabbed Viola Tackett, had confessed to her, for crying out loud. Had stood right there and told her the truth about what happened, about how he had lied to protect himself, moved the body. About how he, Fish, had killed Martha Whittiker, not her druggie grandson, Dylan Shaw.

And Viola Tackett had strung the boy up anyway.

In a staggering conclusion to the nightmare kangaroo court trial, Viola had taken Dylan Shaw out and hung him.

Hung the poor kid from the light pole in front of the courthouse.

After Fish had told her the truth, she had hung Dylan Shaw anyway.

Fish hadn't had a drink since that day, since he'd swayed there in a drunken stupor and watched a sixteen-year-old boy be murdered, be executed for a crime Fish had committed.

Fish hadn't had a drink since.

Not one.

Twelve hours after his final drink, Fish had begun to shake. He was here in the Methodist church basement, where he had run … run as fast and as hard as he could, staggered more likely, all the way from the courthouse. He had not even had to summon willpower to do what he did after he got here. He had been too numb to have responded in any other way.

He had opened every container of alcohol and poured them down the sink in the bathroom. *Everything* — a half a bottle of Smirnoff vodka, a flask of everclear, three bottles of wine, two six-packs of beer and half a bottle of gin. Even the last of the precious Maker's Mark whiskey, the bottle of booze that had been responsible for the death of Martha Whittiker because Holmes had been unwilling to give it back to her ... which had resulted in ... whatever happened.

He'd found himself sobbing in the corner of the room at some point on Sunday but didn't know how he'd gotten there. And the DTs had arrived right on schedule about six o'clock Monday morning.

Nothing as charming as a line of pink elephants like soap bubbles, sparkling and bursting.

He'd vomited until all that was left was his stomach lining. Then kept puking. He'd had the shakes so violently he bit into a wooden pencil to keep his teeth from clacking together. He had started sweating, alcohol sweat that almost smelled the same as pee, he had paced, had cowered in anxiety, had ...

He had done it all.

And even then, even after the best, or the worst, that the DTs could throw at him, he had somehow managed to keep the *real* monsters locked in their cages in the basement of his being.

Until now. Now, when it was worse because they weren't little pink elephant figments of his imagination. Now, when he was sober. Now, Tuesday morning, forty-eight hours after his last drink, after he'd cleaned up the messes he had made in the basement, had even washed the lone "change of clothes" he kept there. They hadn't been a whole lot cleaner than what he was wearing, but after they were washed and dried, they did smell better. He'd taken a shower in the tiny shower in the basement bathroom because he knew he'd feel better if he did that.

And then he planned to go outside, get some fresh air, some sunshine.

He'd gotten a fair distance down the track of that plan when he got run over by a truck. No, he was blessedly free of hallucinations. This wasn't that. Now, he wasn't hallucinating. Now, he was remembering.

The *real* monsters had escaped. They hadn't broken out. They had walked out of *un*locked cages. They were real, you see, and you could only keep them locked up if you were too drunk to recognize their authenticity. You could drown them in booze, could erase them with alcohol.

The booze was gone now, and Holmes Fischer was forced to face the monsters that had started it all.

And so he sat in clothing that was now sweat-stinky again with his back against the concrete wall of the basement of the Methodist church and screamed. Wailed. Shrieked. Cried … and did it all silently. In his head.

A sound penetrated his silent screaming.

A voice.

"Fish … Fish, are you down there?"

He froze.

"Fish, I know you're there. It's me, Charlie McClintock. I need to talk to you."

Still he said nothing.

"I want to ask you about … the Jabberwock."

She said the magic word, and his screams leapt out of his mind and into his throat.

The Jabberwock.

Holmes Fischer screamed and screamed and screamed. Out loud now. Until his throat was raw.

Chapter Nine

Viola and Zach stopped at two houses on the other side of the street from Howie Witherspoon's house and nobody was home. The one on the far end belonged to the Stedmans — Buck and Florence. The house had had a for-sale sign in the yard for … shoot — a year, maybe longer. They finally give up and moved away and left it. The one next to Howie's was Corney Dugger. Cornelius lived by himself, far as she knew, and supposedly worked a factory job somewhere, but that was just what he put out there. He was a drug dealer and last she heard he'd got busted so he was likely in jail somewhere. She'd knocked anyway, though she hadn't seen him since way before J-Day.

Nothing. Only one other place to try.

Zach waited in the car while Viola traipsed across the weedy yard next door to Howie's place and up onto the porch of old man Hayes's house. If anybody'd ever called him anything other than "old man Hayes," Viola hadn't heard it and she didn't know his name.

She hollered out to Zach to "shut that engine off and quit gunning it" and the *vroom-vroom* sound died away.

Just like a little kid …

Viola lifted her fist and banged on the screen door. Waited. Nobody answered. She banged again, louder. It might be the old man was in there but was near onto deaf and couldn't hear her unless she banged on the door with a sledgehammer.

Bam! Bam! Bam!

She hammered on the door with the side of her fist instead of her knuckles.

"Hayes — you in there? Answer the door."

She heard a shuffling sound from inside and the inner door opened a couple of inches, the width of the chain lock. An old man squinted at Viola with rheumy eyes. His hair was thin and wispy, so mussed up it looked like he'd been standing in a wind storm.

"Hep ya?" he asked.

"I'm Viola Tackett," she began.

"Say what? I'm hard of hearing."

"I said, I'm Viola Tackett and—"

"I know who you are. What can I do fer ya?"

"Come to ask about your neighbor, Howie Witherspoon. Where's he at?"

"Howie, you say?"

"Yeah, next door. Howie Witherspoon."

"Don't think he's home." He started to close the door.

"I know he ain't home. That's why I'm here. You know where he's at?"

"You sure he ain't home?

"I done looked."

"Car's there."

"I can see that," Viola snapped. "But Howie ain't there and neither's the boy, Toby's his name. You seen 'em?"

"Nope. I thought they was home. You sure they ain't there?"

This was useless. Viola turned to walk off the porch.

"Might be they left in that van."

Viola stopped and turned around. "What van?"

"I think it was a van. Cain't hardly see nothing but blobs, but it was a white blob bigger'n a car. Figured it must be a van. Or a truck. Might be it was a truck."

"What makes you think Howie left in a van?"

"Van? It mighta been a truck."

Viola ground her teeth but remained calm.

"Truck, then. Why do you think Howie left in a truck?"

"Well, he left in something, didn't he, if he ain't home," the old man snapped. "You think he walked, him with that bad knee?"

Viola fought to control her temper.

"When did you see this truck — or van or whatever — that you think he mighta left in?"

"Yesterday 'fore sunrise. I's up. Don't hardly sleep at all no more. I wouldn't a seen it, but the security light over the garage come on and lit up this white thing in Howie's driveway. Parked behind his car. Can't see hardly nothing in the daylight, but lit up in the dark like that …"

"Did you see Howie or the boy, Toby, get in it?"

"Didn't see nothing. Then the light went off and I went back to bed."

Viola sighed. No help. She turned again to leave.

"Took the dog with 'em. Musta, 'cause it ain't been around in a couple a days. They let it out and it craps in my yard and I can't see it, so I step in it when I go to the mailbox to get the mail. Ain't stepped in nothing since Saturday."

The last time Viola'd seen Howie was Sunday afternoon, when she sent him packing out of the courtroom with the kid. The kid had mentioned the dog. It was the dog that'd dug up his dead mama's purse.

"You see anything else? Anything at all. Think. It's powerful important."

"Nothing but them squiggly lines?"

"Squiggly lines?" Was the old man senile?

"On the side of the truck. Or van. Musta been a van, now that I think about it, because it had squiggly lines on the side."

"Squiggly—"

"Words. They was words written on the side of the thing but I couldn't read it, all I could make out was squiggly lines."

A van with words on the side. There were a couple of those Viola could think of. Joe Stovall had a van, a big cargo thing with the store's logo, Stovall's Used Furniture Store. But it was black, with white lettering. Lester Peetree had a van said Peetree's Hardware Store on the side. It was white. So was E.J.'s. Viola had ridden out to the county line in it on J-Day. It was white and said vet clinic on the side.

"'Preciate yore help," she told the old man and got halfway down the sidewalk when he called after her.

"Fine by me if they don't never come back. Hate the smell of dog crap."

Zach wanted to know what she'd found out but she shushed him, needed to think.

Didn't none of this make sense. Best way to puzzle a thing out was to start with what you did know. She did know Howie wouldn't, *couldn't* have run off somewhere on foot and didn't have no reason to. Somebody took him and the kid somewhere. Maybe in a white van with words on the side. And unless they's going duck hunting, wasn't no reason to leave the house before sunrise — unless they went *in the dark* so wouldn't nobody see.

Might be Howie didn't go willingly.

Who woulda forced him? And why?

She didn't like where this was leading. Didn't like it one bit. But Viola never lied to herself. Couldn't hardly trust nothing that come out of other folks' mouths so you best be able to believe what you told your own self.

"Turn this thing around and take me to the Middle of Nowhere. I need to have a talk with Malachi."

Zach pulled out into the street and laid rubber on the asphalt all the way to the corner.

Chapter Ten

After Charlie called out to Fish from the top step leading down into the basement, he began to scream, to wail, to make noises that didn't even sound human. The sounds scared little Merrie and she yanked backward on her mother's hand.

"Not go there!" she cried, then threw a stranglehold around her mother's leg. "Scares me."

"Scares me, too," Charlie said, and backed away from the steps. She could not take Merrie in there with her, but she needed to talk to Fish. Had to talk to him. And from the sounds he was making, it seemed clear that he needed somebody to take notice of him.

Then the screaming stopped abruptly. Like a spigot turned off. There was silence for a time … then *singing*.

"Thirty-nine bottles of beer on the wall. Thirty-nine bottles of beer. Take one down, pass it around, thirty-eight bottles of beer on the wall. Thirty-eight bottles of beer on the wall, thirty-eight …"

Given the nature of the song, Charlie expected she'd find Fish three sheets to the wind, but as she descended the steps, she noticed that his words were crisp and clear, he wasn't slurring them, and when she caught sight of him, he was sitting at the piano pounding out the music in what appeared to be — oh, please, let it be so — complete sobriety.

The basement was bare of most everything but piles of ancient hymnals, floor to ceiling on one wall, an old upright piano pathetically out of tune on the other with a bench seat in front of it where Fish sat, hammering on the keys and singing at the top of his lungs.

In a far corner was a … nest. A homeless person's nest, consisting of a cot, blankets, a sleeping bag, even a pillow and a couple of shirts and pairs of pants that dangled wet from a makeshift clothesline stretched between water pipes. There was a bathroom in the far corner of the room that Charlie assumed was still functional. The floor was clean, the place was neat and orderly. All things considered, it was a reasonably decent place to live.

She'd glanced in a broken-out window into the church building upstairs and it was clear teenagers had had a grand time in the sanctuary. Graffiti spray-painted on the walls and a pew resting halfway out a broken stained-glass window.

There were no empty liquor bottles in Fish's basement, though, none of the disarray you'd expect from a place occupied by someone in a constant state of inebriation. She stepped into the room without his notice as he banged out his song and howled the words as loud as he could. But there was no way Merrie McClintock could go unnoticed for more than ten seconds at a time and she burst out of Charlie's grip and raced across the room toward the piano bench where Fish sat.

"Mr. Fish, I like dat song!" she cried.

He didn't acknowledge her presence in any way, just

kept at it, with a frenetic quality Charlie had only just noticed.

"Mr. Fish, I play it, too."

The little girl climbed up on the seat beside him and began to bang her hands gleefully on the keys on that end of the piano.

Still Fish didn't notice her.

This was weird. Charlie approached and instantly saw what Merrie had not noticed. Fish's eyes were fixed straight ahead.

And there were tears streaming down his cheeks.

Charlie went to the wall piled high with hymnals.

"Merrie, come here," she called, picking up the top book and opening it. Merrie hopped down off the piano bench and went to her mother.

"I playin' the nano. I makin' music."

"Would you like to make some paper airplanes?"

Merrie's face lit up. "Like da man wiff the cigar?"

Charlie nodded, tore a page out of the hymnal and folded it into a rudimentary paper airplane.

"Like this." She threw it; the paper fluttered to the floor but Merrie didn't know it was supposed to sail so she supposed it had worked just fine.

Charlie ripped out a handful of pages and showered them on the floor at Merrie's feet.

"See if you can make one fly. Or you can wad the paper up into balls and" — Charlie's eyes scanned the room — "see if you can throw them into that trash basket." She thought a moment. "Or you can pretend the books are bricks and you can build a castle with them." That should keep her occupied for a while.

Merrie dropped to her knees and picked up a handful of paper and Charlie crossed to where Fish was banging on the piano.

"Fish ..." she said softly but he didn't respond. She put out her hand and touched his shoulder and then said, for what reason she couldn't have explained, "Mr. Fischer."

Fish froze in place, his hands hanging over the keys. He didn't look at her, just slowly raised his hands, buried his face in them and began to cry softly.

"I didn't mean to," he said through his tears. "It was an accident. I never meant to hurt anybody."

"Hurt who?"

"It was my fault for going there in the first place, though. I had no business there." He turned to her then. "But I told Viola. I stood right there and confessed. And she hanged him anyway." He put his hands back up over his face and continued to cry.

Now Charlie sat frozen in place, trying to fit what Fish had just said into her mind.

Liam had said Dylan Shaw hadn't killed his grandmother. Charlie had tried to defend the boy to Viola ... and earned the wrath of the most dangerous human being in the county. But Viola had ignored her and hung the boy ... even though she *knew* he didn't do it.

Apparently, *Fish* had killed Martha Whittiker, accidentally somehow. He'd confessed, and still Viola had hanged an innocent teenager. Why? Did Dylan Shaw make a more sympathetic victim? Maybe it was because she'd ruled that the boy had done it and she wasn't willing to admit she'd been wrong. Maybe— Charlie stopped herself. No way could she fathom the depths of that woman's depravity. Nobody could. Viola Tackett was a heartless psychopath who would kill anybody who got in her way.

The bottom dropped out of Charlie's belly when she thought about it, though she didn't need what Fish had said to convince her that Viola Tackett absolutely would make good on her threat to kill Charlie if it suited her.

Anytime. Anywhere. There was no safe place in Nowhere County.

Charlie's only hope for survival lay in getting out of here. So did E.J.'s. And maybe even Rusty's.

The Jabberwock. That's what she'd come here to talk to Fish about. When she tuned back into his monologue of grief, she heard him say, "… always getting other people killed. But I didn't know. How could I know? How could anybody know?"

"Know what?"

He took his hands away from his face and looked at her for the first time.

"About the Jabberwock." His eyes were pools of pure misery. "That it could kill people."

Chapter Eleven

Viola instructed Zach to cruise around the Dollar General Store and the back side of the clinic. Sure enough, parked by the back door was a white van with the words Healthy Pets Veterinary Clinic and Hospital on the side. There were no cars parked outside.

"You wait here," she told Zach.

Raylynn Bennett was sitting at the reception desk. She was right pretty for a black girl.

"I come to see Malachi," Viola announced. "Go fetch him for me."

"He's not here."

"Where'd he go — I thought he was living here in E.J.'s apartment."

"He borrowed Charlie's car to go into the Ridge and pick up Reverend Norman."

Which explained why she'd seen the McClintock woman driving Sam's car in the Ridge earlier.

"What was he going to do with the reverend?"

"Take him out to Scott's Ridge to get his car." She

paused. "You know, because that must be where Hayley left it before she ..."

Hayley Norman didn't jump, if that's what Raylynn was about to say. Viola knew what'd happened, and who'd done it. When the preacher found out Howie Witherspoon was the one killed his daughter, Rev. Norman might just decide to head up his own lynch mob.

Except there wasn't no Howie to lynch. And Viola needed to find out what had happened to him. *Exactly* what'd happened to him.

"He say when he'd be back?"

Viola didn't intend to sit here and wait for Malachi. It wasn't in her nature to sit around waiting. Other folks could wait for her.

"No, but he'll have to be here for his shift with E.J."

Just the way she said the words, the look on her face. That girl was heartbroken over what'd happened to the vet. Shoot, maybe E.J. was banging her, too. Who knew?

"When Malachi gets back, you tell him his mama wants him."

A small smile creased Raylynn's lips. "At least you won't have to drag him out of here." The girl realized Viola didn't know what she was talking about. "I'm sorry, I was thinking about Merrie. Charlie's little girl. That kid came in here and took the place over on J-Day. I've never seen a child who loves animals like she does and when her mother comes to get her ..."

Viola turned for the door, but Raylynn's words hung on a nail in her head.

That kid, Merrie.

Viola had seen the little girl the night of the public meeting when she'd had to put Liam down. It'd gone just like she'd planned it until that McClintock woman started mouthing off, talking about people disappearing, getting everybody all up in arms about it.

Truth was, the woman was right. Folks were disappearing. But Viola shied away from that truth as she had seldom shied away from any other. To acknowledge that it was happening, that somehow the Jabberwock was … taking people, was to acknowledge that *she* wasn't in charge. That she wasn't the one calling the shots. It was to acknowledge that sooner or later the Jabberwock would … Viola shoved the thought violently out of her mind and when she did, the image of the little girl returned.

While that Charlie woman and Sam was inside seeing to Liam, Viola had seen the little girl outside playing. She had a June bug tied to a string and was flying it around like it was an airplane. Sarah Throckmorton, the crazy cat lady who looked just like Tweety Bird's grandmother, was helping her.

Sarah Throckmorton. She'd taken the little girl to look after so Charlie could help Sam with Liam. Taken the kid because everybody knew wasn't nobody any better with kids than Sarah Throckmorton.

Kids.

Toby Witherspoon.

Viola stopped outside the door of the clinic but didn't get into the car immediately. She was considering. Let's say Malachi had something to do with Howie's disappearance. He hadn't wanted Viola to give the kid back to his father because he was worried about the boy. As well he should have been. Howie'd killed his wife and he'd likely off the little boy, too, since the kid had fingered him for the murder.

If Malachi and Howie'd had it out over the boy, wasn't no hard thing to figure who'd come out on top. Malachi would have killed Howie in the blink of an eye to save that kid.

Maybe he did. Maybe Malachi killed Howie and that's what'd happened to the man. Howie hadn't run off. He was dead.

Which left the kid, Toby. If Malachi'd killed his daddy, what'd he do with the boy? Had to put him somewhere. Couldn't leave him with Sam or the McClintock woman. Somebody'd see him since they was all the time at the clinic and such.

No, they had to put the kid somewhere out of sight, somewhere wouldn't nobody happen to stumble over him. They needed to leave him with somebody.

Somebody like … oh, maybe Sarah Throckmorton.

It was worth a shot.

Instead of sitting on her butt waiting for Malachi, Viola would go pay a visit to Sarah Throckmorton. Wasn't far, she could be back at the clinic in half an hour. If the kid was there, she'd get him to tell her what'd happened to his daddy. But if the kid was there, she didn't really need to ask. If he was there, Malachi had deposited him there. Which meant Malachi had defied her.

And what was Viola gonna do about *that* if that's what it turned out to be?

Chapter Twelve

SARAH STOOD by the ancient live oak tree, catching her breath, feeling around on the white bun at her neck to rearrange the hairpins that held it there. She had forgotten how much energy it took to look after a child. She'd spent the past quarter of a century since her children moved away — and took her precious grandchildren with them! — with her fur babies, her cats. And they did require a fair amount of care because there were so many of them. Twenty-one altogether — the nineteen who lived with her in the house and the three other feral cats she fed, left bowls for them on the back porch but they were too wild to want to join the family.

But even all of them put together weren't as needy as the boy with the big sad eyes. Poor little Toby Witherspoon. Figured out his father had killed his mother. *Killed her*, and then he barely escaped getting killed by his own father. What must a thing like that do to a little boy not even ten years old?

She could imagine how broken his heart must be. The little chap needed so much love, way more than poor old

Sarah could give him. But she would try, do the best she could!

And the best she could figure to do was to try to keep him busy, keep him doing things so he wouldn't have time to dwell on the loss of his parents.

So they'd come out into the woods this morning to pick blackberries. Sarah knew where there was a lovely blackberry bush up the hill behind her house. She hadn't gone there in a while, what with that Jabberwock thing and all, but it was the primary source of fruit for Sarah's legendary blackberry cobbler. And blackberry preserves. And blackberry pie. And blackberry compote. She already had enough Mason jars full of blackberry-somethings to feed all the blond men in the Norwegian Army, but she'd brought Toby out here today to help her gather more fruit, made it sound to him like she really needed his help, like if he didn't lend her a hand she didn't know how she'd manage to pick all those blackberries all by herself.

She knew little boys, had raised four of them by herself, along with three girls, after Arnie passed. She knew didn't nothing build a fire under them faster than believing they were helping out, that somebody needed them.

Picking fruit would occupy his time, keep him from thinking about sad things. Keeping him from being afraid of Viola Tackett!

Sam had explained it all to her when she'd dropped Toby at Sarah's house, said she would completely understand if Sarah didn't want to get mixed up in something like that, crossing Viola Tackett. Said she would find somebody else to look after Toby if—

And Sarah'd set her straight quick. Of course, she would look after the poor dear little boy. And no, she was *not* afraid of crossing Viola Tackett. Pooh on Viola Tackett. What was the worst the woman could do to her? Did Sam think Sarah Throckmorton was afraid to die? Pooh. Of course, she was ready to meet her maker. Had been ready for years. Wasn't nothing Viola Tackett could do to scare Sarah Throckmorton.

Well, except hurt Toby. That was the thing. Sarah didn't give a hoot about that loudmouthed Tackett woman, but Sam made it clear that if she found Toby ... it wouldn't be good. She didn't go into details about why but she didn't have to. Viola had released Toby's father even after she knew he'd killed Toby's mother, had given the boy back to him!

Sarah understood that agreeing to look after Toby also meant agreeing to hide him, to keep Viola Tackett from finding him.

Toby came running up to her with her blackberry bucket only half full, his face creased with fear.

"Somebody pulled into your driveway," he said, pointing through the trees and down the hill to her house. "It looks like that lady judge, the one that ... you know, the one that—"

"She see you?"

"No. I jumped behind the blackberry bush."

"Good for you."

Sarah couldn't see well enough to know who it was who'd pulled into her driveway. Cataracts. Doctor told her about them a couple of years ago and she kept meaning to go have something done about them. He said they could take 'em off, help her see better. And she meant to do it, she really did. Just one thing and then another come up, and it was hard to get somebody to take care of so many cats while she was gone and she just never got around to it.

She wished now she had, wished she could *see*.

Well, the boy could see. They'd go with that.

"You think she came here looking for ... me?"

"Don't care why she come. Don't like that woman. Never have. Even if she just come to borrow a cup of sugar, I ain't talking to her." She gestured toward the deeper woods behind them. Even if Sarah couldn't see more than three feet in front of her face, she could find her way around in these woods. She'd come squirrel hunting with Arnie when they'd first built the house half a century ago. She usta come looking for her boys, switch in her hand because one or the other of them was about to get their backsides tanned, she'd looked for blackberries and mushrooms and hunted ginseng. Wasn't an inch of the woods Sarah Throckmorton didn't know.

She took Toby's hand and told him, "We about to hide so good we won't even be able to find our own selves."

And the two of them slipped into the shadows between the trees and vanished.

Chapter Thirteen

Zach pulled his fancy black car into the driveway of Sarah Throckmorton's house and screeched to a halt in front of the garage door.

Took Viola a minute to catch her breath.

Wasn't no reason to be flying down the road like his pants was on fire, but Zach was having a grand ole time acting like a five-year-old. Soon's he stopped the car, Viola reached over and whacked him hard on the shoulder.

"What?" he wailed plaintively. "You said you was in a hurry."

"You don't want to get on my last nerve, you hear me, boy? You surely don't want to do that for a fact."

He seen she meant business then.

"You take one more corner too fast, fling me up against this door, and it will be the last time you get behind the wheel of this car or any other. You understand what I'm saying to you? I will run this car off the top of Chisolm Bluff and watch it tumble all the way down into Troublesome Creek.

"Yes ma'am," he said. Sounded like a kid caught with

his hand in the cookie jar. It totally confounded Viola how conflicted that always made her feel, seeing him cow before her like he done. Oh, she wanted her boys to do what she told 'em, wanted 'em to toe the line. Course she did. But dagnabit, she would dearly love to see one of them stand up on his hind legs and act like a man. Like he had some stones. Just once. Only one of them wasn't a weak-willed, lily-livered pansy was … Malachi.

Malachi didn't take nothing off nobody. Never did. Not even his own mother.

So what was she going to do if he really did defy her, if he done something to Howie after she expressly told him to leave Howie be? Oh, she could make good on her threat to off the McClintock woman. But that wasn't it. What would she do if Malachi really was … *on the other side?* Really did intend to stand up to her, refuse to bow to her authority as the person in charge of the county?

Could she …?

Malachi?

Do something to Malachi?

She shook it off. One step at a time.

Right now, she wasn't a hundred percent sure she wouldn't see Howie Witherspoon and his kid walking down Main Street fit as fiddles.

She wouldn't, of course. But she wasn't sure. She would forestall all what-if's and what'll-I-do-with-Malachi, *to*-Malachi-if … until she knew exactly what'd happened.

Sarah Throckmorton was a shot in the dark, of course. She might not know Jack about Howie or the boy. But it wasn't like Viola had anywhere else to look.

The house was a right pretty little thing, reminded Viola of them stories in kiddie books about gingerbread houses in the woods. It was white, looked freshly painted but that was just because it had aluminum siding and it didn't need painting. It grew that green moss stuff up on the sides, though, but apparently Sarah kept that cleaned off.

Had a regular old picket fence and a gate. And cats all over the yard. The place was plum broke out with the critters.

There was two big, fat cats lying on a rug in the sun on the porch, a black one was perched on top of one of the fence posts. How did cats do stuff like that, anyway, hop up onto the top of things and sit there like hood ornaments? She opened the gate and two or three cats came her way — a calico and two white ones but she kicked out at them to shoo them off. Viola didn't mind a dog now and then but she couldn't stomach cats.

"Get on away from me," she growled and the animals backed up. She left the two sunning on the porch and stepped up to the door, knocked loud.

Nobody answered.

She knocked again. Still nothing.

Wasn't no car in the driveway, but it could be in the garage. Where did a woman like Sarah Throckmorton have to go? All her kin had moved off, or so Viola thought.

She opened the screen door, knocked, called out, "Anybody here?" and tried the doorknob. it wasn't locked, of course, so she went inside. Sarah Throckmorton was nowhere to be found, and Viola would've dearly loved to chat with that woman. Viola hadn't found 'xactly what she was looking for, but she mighta found out what she wanted to know. Maybe.

A loaf of homemade bread sat wrapped in plastic in the middle of the kitchen table, with crumbs around it. A jar of homemade jam sat beside it and the plastic tablecloth was sticky, like a gob of jam had been dropped on it but not cleaned up proper. A bread knife lay beside *two* clean plates in the kitchen dish drainer and *two* glasses.

Viola poked around in the bedrooms — beds was made, but in the small one off the den, she found a baseball cap hung on the bedpost. It was a Cincinnati Reds hat, a small one — about the size a boy like Toby woulda wore — Toby and a couple dozen other little boys she could think of.

Still, her gut yanked into a knot when she seen it. She'd been driven forward by curiosity and anger. Didn't nobody defy Viola Tackett and live to tell the tale. But somehow, some part of her managed to believe that she was wrong about the whole thing. That Howie Witherspoon had gone off somewhere with his kid and his going didn't have nothing to do with her Malachi. Nothin' a'tall.

But it was clear there was a kid here, a little boy. And if that little boy was Toby Witherspoon, then Sarah was looking after him 'cause he didn't have no daddy.

And if he didn't have no daddy, wasn't but one thing coulda happened to him.

She clutched the baseball cap in her hand, marched out the front door with it and got in the car.

"We going back to the Middle of Nowhere. And go on ahead. Let 'er rip. Drive fast as you want. Me'n yore little brother need to have us a talk *right now!*"

Chapter Fourteen

"Moses, this is Jolene Rutherford and I have to talk to you." The message was one of three his machine had recorded while he had been at the grocery store yesterday afternoon. He got so few messages he hadn't even noticed the little red light blinking until this morning. And when he listened to this one, he didn't bother with the other two. "I'm going to sound like a raving lunatic, but Moses, I need your help. I … I've hit the jackpot — ghosts. Ghost*s* — plural. Not one, not even a dozen. I don't know how many. Real. I'm not sure I believed there was such a thing, not even after all the conversations with you. There are real ghosts here, and that's not even the most important part. Moses, the whole county has vanished, I don't know how many people. Nobody knows how many there were here to start with but there's not a soul here now. They're all gone. Vanished. Nothing but empty houses. I don't think they're all dead — they're not. My father is one of them, his house is … I know I'm sounding crazier every second, but please, call me. I don't know what to do when it's real. Please … help me find my father."

Moses Habakuk Weiss locked the door of his little shop behind him and went out to his car parked on the street out front. He looked back at the building once and saw his own reflection in the window — a bent old man, a hundred years old if he was a day — beneath the words "Craftsman Cobbler, shoe repairs, insoles, shoelaces."

Beneath that: "A journey of a thousand miles begins with a single step." Lao Tzu, 4th Century A.D.

And beneath that: "Every journey *seems* like a thousand miles if your feet hurt." Moses Weiss, 1945.

He'd thought that was a nice touch. His Flossie had not agreed. She thought it was, what was it she said? Cheesy. Yes, cheesy. And she reminded him that she thought so every day for thirty-five years. He multiplied it out once, got the grand total of days he'd listened to her litany of things she said every day. If she'd lived another couple of years, it would have been near twenty thousand.

You missed a spot shaving. And its variation, *you have shaving cream under your ear.*

Smile once in a while, it won't break your face.

Collect payment up front. If they don't pay — hold their wingtips hostage until they do.

Flossie was so much nicer dead than she'd ever been alive. Over the years, he'd discovered that a whole lot of people were like that.

Jolene had been nice alive, though, always nice to him even when others weren't. He'd met her when she'd brought in that pair of Christian Louboutin red sole ankle-wrap sandals with a broken buckle. He never forgot a pair of shoes. He'd wondered since then if the shoes had just been an excuse, if she'd heard about him on the grapevine and wanted to come check him out. He'd almost asked once, but didn't because he knew she'd tell him the truth and he didn't really want to know it'd been a setup. That part didn't matter now.

"They're all gone. Vanished. Nothing but empty houses. Please … help me find my father."

That'd been the kicker. He would not ever have written Jolene Rutherford off as a lunatic. She was absolutely sane — shrewd, calculating and manipulating, things you had to be sane to pull off.

But even if he'd thought she was crazy, he wouldn't have written her off and she knew that. He didn't write anybody off. Not with the things his old eyes had seen in his seventy-three years on the earth. He knew, understood on a gut level, a soul level, that absolutely anything was possible.

"Help me find my father…"

There was such terror in her voice, such desperation. Whatever "reality" might be in this situation, it was absolutely true that Jolene was a desperate, frightened woman. Moses Weiss could read people. Of course, he could. When a man's dead wife was whispering in your ear that a fellow was lying when he looked sincere, or was sincere when he looked like he was lying, after a while you learned how to recognize the tells even without the whispered teleprompter.

He opened the back door to his car, tossed his suitcase inside, closed the door. Opened it again, closed it. Opened it again, closed it. Then he just stood there.

He couldn't do this, of course. Absolutely could not.

He could be walking into the belly of the beast. And this time … *this time,* he knew in his bones he would never come back.

No, not this time. He would not rush to the aid of the damsel in distress.

You got a savior complex, you know that, don't you? Your mother, may she rest in peace, never should have named you Moses.

He turned and walked hurriedly back to his shop, fit the key in the lock from the set of keys so ginormous it sometimes took him five minutes to find the one he was looking for. But the shop key was marked with a faded dollop of pink fingernail polish.

All those keys — what, you're the warden in a prison and you have a key for every cell?

He walked through the door and closed it behind him. Opened it again and closed it. And again. He hung his raincoat and hat on the hook by the door and walked behind the counter and put on the black apron he wore because … because he always wore it. Cobblers wore aprons. They just did. He glanced out through the front window, where all the words were backwards from the inside, and saw his car parked on the street.

He had put his suitcase in the car.

He walked to the door.

It was supposed to rain.

He reached up and took his hat and raincoat off the hook and put them on, stepped outside, went to the car, opened the back door and started to get his suitcase out. Paused.

He really ought to help Jolene.

He didn't want to.

The degree to which he didn't want to do it ought to indicate how badly he needed to because the really hairy ones were always preceded by resistance.

Okay, he'd go.

He went back to the door of his shop, opened and closed it three times, locked it, then got into his car and drove all the way to the corner before he turned around and pulled back into the space in front of the shop. But this time, he merely had the argument with himself in the car, lost, and pulled back out again.

He only changed his mind one more time before he got on the expressway, Interstate 75 north to Kentucky.

He was still wearing his black apron.

But that was okay. After all, Moses Weiss was a cobbler.

Chapter Fifteen

Viola marched in the front door of the veterinary clinic loaded for bear. On her way to the clinic she'd washed through all kinda different emotions. Some of them was real different from what she normally felt. She felt sad, betrayed. And her feelings was hurt. Of course, she was madder'n dammit, too, and she went with that one because it was a familiar emotion, felt comfortable as slipping the bunions on her old foot into a worn and comfy house shoe. When she got her hands on Malachi, she was gonna shake the truth out of him and—

Raylynn wasn't sitting at the reception desk and wasn't one of them bell things on the counter to ring to summon her. 'Sides, Viola didn't feel like waiting for nobody. Raylynn was back in the back, in E.J.'s room, likely, so Viola marched through the connecting door and into the hallway, looking for her in each of the rooms as she passed them.

In the second one on the right, she heard a sound coming from under the door and burst into the room without bothering to knock.

It wasn't E.J.'s room, though. Sam Sheridan sat in a chair beside a bed with a young boy stretched out on it. it was her boy, Rusty was his name. Viola had heard about how that Looney Tune Claire McFarland had gone nuts when her kid showed up in the Middle of Nowhere after he got bit by a rattlesnake, heard the crazy woman had gone down to Bascum's and snatched the corpse of her kid out of the funeral home. There was more to the story, something about her kidnapping Sam's boy for some reason, that Malachi'd had to coldcock that McFarland woman because she was holding a shotgun on the lot of them.

But she didn't know Sam's boy'd been hurt.

And clearly he had, because the sound she'd heard from outside in the hallway was somebody crying. Sam.

Sam sat frozen now, staring at Viola, and Viola suspected she might have been the last person in the world Sam expected to see in her son's hospital room. Viola felt uncharacteristically uncomfortable about storming in like she done. Sam Sheridan was … well, didn't nobody in the county have nothing against that woman. Viola certainly wouldn't have bothered her if she'd knowed—

"What are you … what do you want?" Sam stammered, as she quickly wiped the tears off her cheeks, like she was embarrassed somebody'd caught her crying. No, not embarrassed. More like … and then Viola got it. Sam didn't want nobody to see her cry because she was in charge. She had to be strong even if she didn't feel like it because they was folks counting on her. Viola got it because she knew what it felt like to be the one calling the shots, the one everybody looked to to know what to do … so you had to act like you knew even if you didn't have no idea.

"Sorry," Viola heard herself say. Couldn't remember

the last time she'd apologized for anything. "Didn't mean to come storming in like that." She drew herself up, tried to summon the anger and indignation that had propelled her but it had dissipated when she stepped into the room and saw Sam sitting by the hospital bed crying.

The room had obviously been converted from a storage room into a hospital room. It had no windows and there were boxes stacked against the far wall. In fact, it seemed more like somebody's bedroom than a hospital room. The kid was lying on his side on a half bed, not a hospital bed. There was a table beside the bed that had a lamp on it, not a hospital room lamp but one out of a living room, with a brass base and a lampshade. The shade softened the light, so that the illumination fell in a gentle glow out from it and across the youngster lying so still on the white sheet.

And something happened to Viola when she looked at the boy, really *saw* him.

His face was pale, almost as white as the crisp pillowcase where his head lay. His hair was tousled on his forehead, brown hair but there were hints of his mother's red hair in the glow of the lamplight.

He was a handsome boy, would be a heartthrob one of these days, would have to beat the girls off with a stick just like her Malachi.

And then Viola Tackett lost her breath.

She couldn't breathe when an image burst into her mind, leapt right front and centerstage with a bright light shining on it. It was perfect in every detail, as clear as one of them pictures from a fancy camera that had lenses you could take off and change. Crisp. Not a memory because memories weren't that clear. It was an image that had dragged a moment from the past into the center of her mind and lit it up hot and stinking in the middle of it.

Viola stood as frozen as a grave stone.

"… do you want?"

Sam's words came from a long way off, from the bottom of a well where the water was so far down you could barely hear a plunk sound when you tossed in a rock.

Viola looked at Sam, took in her face as if it were the face of a stranger, looked at it the way you look at someone you just met. She looked from Sam to the boy — Rusty. His name was Rusty. That hair was the thing, the color of rust. Not red like his mother's but darker. As if the red had been stirred together with black and the mixed color — neither black nor red but some color that was both and neither. The color of rust.

"… want here?"

Viola heard the words and listened to them now, not because the distracting image had left her mind but because it had settled down there, snuggled in warm and comfortable in a spot where it fit perfectly.

"I'm … looking for Malachi. You seen him?"

Her words were like them words that come out of a doll without no feeling in them, like a recording.

"He left a while ago in Charlie's car to take Reverend Norman out to Scott's Ridge. Reverend Norman thinks—"

"Thinks his Hayley was there before she got beat to death. Yeah, I heard. What's wrong with him?"

Sam was confused. "Wrong with who? Reverend Norman?"

"No, him." She gestured at the boy on the bed. "What happened?"

She could see the question hit Sam like a blow to the belly.

"He … Claire McFarland … *shot him!*" There was steel rage in those two words and Viola would have expected nothing less. "In the back … with a shotgun. The buckshot almost … it peeled all the skin off!"

"That ain't all, though, is it?" Viola had turned back to look at the boy on the bed. "What's the rest of it?"

"She forced him to … she shoved him into the Jabberwock and he came back here."

Viola's head snapped toward Sam.

"You saying he rode the Jabberwock a *second* time?"

Sam just nodded, didn't say the words out loud. Maybe couldn't.

"He gonna be alright, ain't he?" It was less a question than a demand.

Sam looked at her, as surprised as Viola was by her words. Viola watched her struggle, saw her quash the knee-jerk, he'll-be-fine response and replace it with the truth.

"I … don't know." She spoke the next words in a whisper full of desperation. "He needs a doctor! He could have … brain damage."

"No, he ain't," Viola barked. "He ain't got nothing of the kind. That boy's gonna be fine, just fine. You'll see."

Sam's head snapped toward her and their eyes locked and held. Something escaped from Sam in that moment that didn't need no words to say it. Viola was sure Sam was unaware the knowing had got away from her, didn't know it had broke out of that place deep in the dark where she kept it.

Viola stopped breathing again. Couldn't a'drawn a breath even if it was her last one on this earth.

She didn't say another word. Couldn't. Just turned on her heel and strode out of the room, back down the hallway — brushing past Raylynn without even asking about Malachi — across the waiting room, out the door to the car.

When she slammed the car door shut, Zach asked, "We goin' home, Mama?"

"Yeah, home." Then she shook her head. "Not in town, not to the Nower House." She heard the slip-up but didn't care. "We going home to Turkey Neck Hollow. You get us to Chicken Gizzard Ridge *fast*, boy, fast as you can. There's something there I got to see."

Chapter Sixteen

After Malachi's fourth week in boot camp at Marine Corps Training Camp Lejeune in Jacksonville, North Carolina, the grunts — as the shaved-headed recruits were called — were allowed to watch old movies and old tv shows in the rec room off the commissary on Friday nights, and it was there that he was introduced to classic shows he had never seen because he had grown up in a home that had no television set. The grunts hooted and howled at the absurd "special effects" of the old science fiction movies. Malachi was particularly fond of the robot on *Lost in Space* with arms that looked like the hoses that connected clothes driers to outside vents, with pincher hands like ice tongs on the ends. He loved it when the robot lit up like a pinball machine and announced in a monotone, "Danger! Danger! Danger, Will Robinson."

The moment the Pentecostal church minister slid into the front seat beside Malachi in Charlie's borrowed car, all Malachi's gut instincts, trained combat instincts, all his 'marine's sixth sense' instincts sounded the same alarm as that robot. All of them were bleating *Danger! Danger! Danger!*

Something was very, very wrong with Duncan Norman.

"Good morning, Reverend Norman," he said. The man turned eyes as hard as granite on him and said nothing, just bobbed his head in the barest acknowledgement.

Okay, fine. The man just lost his only daughter. Sam said he'd refused to take her advice to remember his daughter as the girl in the picture in his wallet — and had rushed to Bascum's to see the girl's body. Malachi had seen it when Skeeter Burkett had lifted the tarp off it in the back of Ed Reynolds's pickup truck and had helped carry the body into the basement of the funeral home and lay it on the tray of one of the refrigeration drawers. It was as gristly a sight as Malachi had ever seen on a battlefield, a body that'd been tossed into a river off a 600-foot cliff after being beaten beyond recognition.

Murdered by Howie Witherspoon.

Had to be. Howie had shown up in the courtroom Sunday afternoon looking like he'd been kicked in the face … with the kind of combat boot Hayley'd been wearing when she was fished out of the river. A broken nose, black eyes, missing teeth and an injured thumb Malachi would bet had been bitten. And most important, four telltale scratches — gouges down his left cheek. Claw marks, the signature of a woman with long fingernails. He'd noticed Hayley's — brightly painted stick-on nails and one on her right hand had been broken off.

He hadn't asked Toby any questions — didn't want to traumatize the poor kid any worse than he already had been, but the boy had babbled out his story, obviously needed to talk about it as Malachi had driven him to take refuge at Sam's house the night after Malachi's mother had hanged an innocent teenager from a lamp post in front of the courthouse. It'd been the same horrifying tale

Toby'd told to Viola in court — of watching his father beat his mother, "careful not to leave bruises where they'd show" and then she'd vanished and his father had said she'd gone shopping in Lexington and was trapped outside the county by the Jabberwock. But Toby said she had been home that day, and had presented Viola his mother's purse that the dog had dug up out of the compost heap as proof that she "wouldn't have gone shopping without her credit cards."

Clearly, Howie had killed his wife. But Viola had set him free and given Toby back to him, after warning the boy not to keep "telling them lies" about his father. If Malachi hadn't intervened, hadn't killed Howie as he held a knife to the boy's throat, Howie would have murdered Toby, too.

And as they'd ridden through the darkness that night, Toby had expanded on his tale of horror, described how he'd overheard his father talk "like he was mad" to someone he called "Hayley" on the phone Saturday afternoon, arranged to meet her. About being left all alone — trying not to be scared — until his father came home Saturday night injured and bloody. Howie had been having sex with a teenage girl, got her pregnant, and when she couldn't get an abortion, he had murdered her.

Now, Malachi sat in strained silence beside the girl's father, driving him out to Scott's Ridge overlook to pick up the car Hayley'd left there before she died. Before he'd picked Duncan up at his house, Malachi had been considering whether or not he ought to share with the man what he knew about his daughter's murder. But that would beg the question: where was Howie Witherspoon now? Duncan Norman would want to know, would demand justice ... and justice had already been served. Malachi had carried out the death sentence to save Toby ... but if Viola found out he'd done that, she'd pronounce her own death sentence on Charlie.

It was all so convoluted and complicated. Every action set off a domino effect that cascaded danger everywhere the dominoes fell.

Malachi couldn't tell Duncan what he knew, at least not now. It would put Charlie's life in danger. And besides, right now, Duncan Norman didn't look like a man able to process information like that. He looked like a man on a razor's edge of … insanity.

Giving up any effort to make small talk with the minister, Malachi stole sidelong looks at the man as he drove down Wiley Road north out of the Ridge, then onto Crockett Pike to Bent Creek Road, which wound up the side of Ironwood Mountain and then down into Chicory Hollow. The nameless road that provided access to the Scott's Ridge Overlook, with its panoramic view across the Rolling Fork River into Dragonroot Hollow, was just "the overlook road."

Duncan Norman was handsome in an austere, aristocratic way, reminded Malachi of the actor Gregory Peck, whose face bore solemnity more comfortably than a smile. Malachi certainly wouldn't expect Duncan Norman to be smiling now — he had never seen a man so tense — not even going into a firefight. The minister was strung as tight as the high-note keys on a piano. Malachi'd looked into the back of a piano once, saw the wires stretched tight that the little hammers struck to make music notes. The shortest wires, the ones strung the tightest of all, were the ones attached to the keys on the far right side of the instrument. Duncan Norman was a man whose whole being could produce only high notes.

Even that was *off*, though. He wasn't upset, mourning, devastated. He appeared to be … angry. Yes, there was raging fury, boiling hatred barely held in check behind his eyes. That was perhaps an understandable response to the murder of your daughter … but it was more than that. More focused and directed than blind rage. Duncan Norman's whole carriage and demeanor radiated … what? *Danger!* Like heat pulsing off a wood stove. Malachi could sense it. Could smell it.

The man seated beside him was as perilous as a ticking IED. And somehow Malachi couldn't register that as "understandable" in his mind.

Something was wrong. Very, very wrong. Waves of danger lapped against Malachi's instincts. And he had no idea what it was.

He pulled Charlie's car into a secluded parking lot in the trees. The scenic overlook faced due west, surrounded on three sides by forest. The lot was north of the overlook, connected to it by a winding pathway that meandered through a quarter mile of woods. As expected, there was a car parked there, an old Ford. Malachi didn't ask if it was Duncan Norman's car because it was clear from the look on his face that it was. What else was clear from the look on his face was that the sight of it had primed the fuse. He was just about to blow.

Malachi wondered what form the explosion would take, but suspected whatever it was, it was going to be ugly. Maybe Duncan had known this was how it'd be and that's why he'd asked a stranger to accompany him. Perhaps he really didn't want any members of his congregation to watch him lose it and become completely hysterical.

Or worse.

Malachi drove behind the Ford and pulled into the space beside it, put the car in park and killed the engine. And looked at Duncan Norman.

The man didn't move, just sat staring straight ahead.

Malachi opened his door and got out, walked around the back of the car and into the space between it and the Ford. Duncan got out and closed the car door behind him and stood looking at the driver's side of his own car.

As soon as Malachi got close, he saw it, too.

Oh, no.

Malachi's heart sank.

It would be no simple thing for Duncan Norman to get into his car and drive away. There was dried blood all over the driver's side door, on the handle, dripping in a dried rivulet down the side of the car and all over the driver's side window.

Malachi looked through the bloody window and saw a white leather purse sitting in the passenger seat. It was the kind that snapped shut at the top and it was standing open, with dried blood stains all over it. Howie had obviously come to Hayley's car after he killed her, wanted something out of her purse, and had smeared her blood and his all over everywhere.

How could Rev. Norman just ... get into the bloody car and drive away? Maybe Malachi could clean some of it off. Maybe Charlie had something in her car — a towel or something he could use to wipe the blood off — at least off the door handle. He turned back toward Charlie's car and saw Duncan had moved, had backed away after he closed the car door. He had stopped beside the front bumper of the car. He was holding a pistol that he raised and leveled at Malachi's chest.

The man spoke then for the first time, let loose a torrent of obscenities Malachi was surprised he even knew. He spit the words out as if each one tasted unimaginably foul in his mouth and they rode a wave of rage the man vomited out into the air between them.

Not sentences. Individual words and phrases. He was

sputtering, spittle flying out at Malachi, his eyes so wild the pupils were dilated like he was on drugs. But his hands on the pistol were firm. The barrel didn't shake. He held it in a two-hand grip out in front of him while he shrieked.

Malachi finally gathered sense from the nonsensical ravings.

Duncan Norman believed *Malachi* had killed Hayley. And he would become the Lord's righteous hand of retribution, delivering justice. An eye for an eye.

Malachi had maybe five seconds before the man opened fire and put a bullet in his chest. He had to disarm him, but Malachi needed a distraction, a moment of inattention.

Then he noticed the handprint.

Chapter Seventeen

Neb hitched the belt of his pants up and fastened the buckle tighter in the front. His belly hung out over the buckle, so it was hard to fasten. Then he fit the gun belt on top of his own belt and fastened it there.

The whole apparatus was so tight he could barely draw in a breath. But if he wore the gun belt low over his hips down beneath his belly, the holsters attached to it were too far down the outside of his thigh for him to reach the guns properly.

Quick-drawing was turning out to be more complicated than Neb Tackett had thought it would be.

"Ahhh-nah, gahma-gahma-gahma, so-so-wissy-wheeee."

Essie sat on the top step of the front porch, smoothing back the ratty hair of the Barbie doll she played with, singing that song that wasn't no song to soothe herself, the two middle fingers on her right hand stuck in her mouth with that fat tongue so wasn't nothing but garbled sound come out.

Essie was why he had to practice in the front yard of the house rather than in the back like he done earlier. He had to be where Essie could see him or she'd get upset and start crying. Or what passed for crying — rocking back and forth with her arms wrapped tight around herself, making a wheezy, whistling, mewling sound with tears running down her cheeks.

Essie was only content sitting on the *front porch* of the Nower House. Zach and Obie'd had to carry her upstairs to bed last night and Mama'd had put a pillowcase over her head to blindfold her and lead her down one step at a time back downstairs this morning.

Neb sat back down on the bottom step below Essie, checking each one of the guns, running his fingers lovingly over the pearl handles and feeling the cold metal of the barrel. Neb felt about guns the way Zach felt about cars. He loved everything about them, from how a pistol fit snug in the palm of his big hand to what happened when you pulled the trigger — the violence, the destruction, the domination and triumph. He had *never* owned pistols as fine as these, though. He'd have preferred a single-action revolver, one that had to be thumb-cocked in order to fire. The trigger pull on a single-action could be real light, since you done all the mechanical work with your thumb when you cocked it. Specifically, he coveted a Colt Single-Action Army revolver, known as the Model 1873 Revolver — called the "Peacemaker." *That* was the pistol they used in all the old cowboy movies.

The pistols he'd stole from Peetree's Hardware were double-action revolvers, Smith & Wesson Model 10s. You could cock one before you fired it, but you didn't have to. Just pulling the trigger rotated the cylinder to bring up a fresh cartridge, and drove the hammer all the way back, then dropped it to fire the gun. Single-action pistols was more accurate than double-action 'cause you didn't have to yank so hard on the trigger to make them fire.

Neb hadn't never fired neither one of these pistols, had to figure a way to go out somewhere by himself so Mama wouldn't hear the shots. He flipped open the chambers of the first one, then the other, spun the chambers around, making sure every slot had a round. When he'd gotten out the box of the shells to load them, he'd tried to fit extra shells into the slots for them on the gun belt. He didn't understand that part — the single bullet slits in the gun belt. He tried to force the shells one at a time into the slits, finally got one in but with his big fingers it was almost impossible to work it back out again. In a gunfight, it'd be a whole lot easier to re-load from a handful of bullets in his pocket, rather than trying to pull the bullets out of the belt slits.

But he'd stopped trying to fit the bullets into the slits, didn't grab a handful of shells to put in his pocket neither 'cause he wasn't gonna to be in no gunfight. Wouldn't need but one bullet. That's all it would take to put down the El Dorado Kid. If it wasn't for the Jabberwock, Neb woulda gone up Lexington and got hisself a Stetson hat and some gen-u-ine Tony Lama boots. Now, he had to make do with a John Deere cap pulled low over his eyes and his work boots.

He got slowly to his feet, patted the guns on each hip, set his jaw and stepped away from the porch where Essie sat singing her song.

"Ghamma, gamma, soooooo, so-wissy," the words somewhere between a chant and a melody.

. . .

Lily has come out of the saloon to the wooden sidewalk as Tack shows the little boy his guns.

"You go on home now, son," Tack tells the boy, before spinning each of the pistols around his finger and fitting it back into its holster. "Get inside and stay there."

The boy turns and runs away down the sidewalk as fast as he can, his boots clunking lightly on the wooden sidewalk.

Tack looks at Lily, holds the gaze of her violet eyes, nods, then steps down off the wooden sidewalk and walks slowly down the street, moving with the grace of a big cat, each step kicking up a puff of dust from the street.

His arms hang limp at his sides. He flexes his fingers, then relaxes his hands.

"Hey, Kid," he calls out. "I hear you're looking for me." He takes two more long strides. "Well, here I am. Come and get me. Unless you've turned chicken and run."

No one replies and Tack takes two more steps.

"Oh, I ain't run, sheriff," says a voice.

And Tack freezes. The voice has come from behind him. *As if he has eyes in the back of his head, Tack can see the sniveling coward standing on the sidewalk — with Lily held in front of him as a shield.*

"Tack, don't—" Lily cries, but her words are cut off.

"What's the matter, sheriff? Afraid I'm too fast for ya?"

Tack knows what he must do. He must spin, draw and fire — in one motion faster than lightening and his aim must be perfect because Lily is …

He begins to turn, his movements smooth, fast and flawless. He grabs the Colt out of the holster on his right hip with his left hand, and the one on his left hip with—

Bang!

The sound of the gunshot so startled Neb that he

dropped the gun out of his left hand and released his hold on the half-drawn gun in his right. That gun flew out of the holster and banged into the bottom of the railing around the front porch and dropped with a thud into the tall grass.

Whew! The trigger on that pistol was so light he pulled it just grabbing it out of the holster! Double-action was supposed to be way stiffer than that. Must be because this was such a fine weapon that—

He heard an odd sound. Like the whine of a dog.

Lifting his eyes then to the top step of the porch, he was surprised that Essie wasn't sitting there no more. Where—?

Then he realized she was still there, she just wasn't *sitting*. She was lying on her back on the porch with her feet still resting on the next step down.

Why did …?

Then Neb was standing over her and he had no memory at all of moving. He had been standing with the guns lying in the grass at his feet and then he was standing on the porch looking down at Essie.

She lay there looking up at him. But she didn't have that blank, stupid look on her face, like wasn't nothing at all going on in her head.

Now she was looking at him … confused. Surprised.

She lifted her hand like she was going to reach out to him, but then let her hand drop to her chest. The limp hand plopped down on top of the smear of red on the front of her tee shirt, a swatch of crimson that was spreading out from the center.

It took Neb several seconds to figure out what was going on, to understand why Essie was lying on her back on the porch.

When he figured it out, his legs went out from under

him, and he folded up at the knee. His un-hinged legs dumped him on the porch beside the bleeding body of his sister.

Bleeding from the gunshot wound the bullet from a Smith & Wesson Model 10 had put in her chest.

Chapter Eighteen

VIOLA DIDN'T SAY nothing to Zach about him driving too fast so he kept the pedal to the metal all the way out Route 17 South to Gallagher Station Road, past the Killarney cutoff and into Turkey Neck Hollow to Farmer's Branch Road that jigged and jawed along the side of Gizzard Ridge. He'd had to slow down then, it not even being paved and all. They passed by the Martins' house at the bottom of the hill and Eunice was out working in her garden. She threw up her hand to wave hidy and Zach waved back. Viola hardly noticed her at all. Her mind was in other places, making connections. Wondering as she watched the cabin come into view as they passed beyond the last tree.

It was a simple, ugly log home — added to over the years as the need arose, as worn out and used up as Viola sometimes felt. Zach pulled right up in front of the house and stopped, didn't gun the engine in a vroom, vroom, though Viola could tell he wanted to, just knew better. He sat looking at her, but didn't say nothing. Also a good idea on his part.

It seemed like she hadn't been here in a hundred years, when in truth she'd only kicked Sebastian Nower out of *her* house on Sunday morning and today was Tuesday. The mere passage of time didn't explain how she felt. And neither did the "wonky" Jabberwock time. Oh, she'd noticed it, alright. Of course she had. Anybody with a pulse had figured out by now that time locked inside Nowhere County by the mirage on the border wasn't the same's it had been before. Neither was the weather — the temperature, no clouds. And the sky with its un-sparkling stars. She hadn't mentioned it to nobody because what was the point. It was what it was. It was all messed up and the Jabberwock had done it and wasn't nothing to be said about it one way or the other. She refused to allow herself to speculate on what other things the Jabberwock had the power to do if it could control the sky and the weather. Like maybe making houses old overnight. Or making people vanish.

Yeah, that part was happening, too, just like that Charlie woman had said at the town meeting. Only a fool would argue with a thing like that when the proof was right there before your eyes. The Furmans' house. The Blakes'. Others. All of them suddenly falling-down shacks.

Viola seen it but wouldn't grant the knowing of it to take up space in her mind. That, too, was what it was and wasn't no sense 'lowing a thing you couldn't change or fix park itself in your head and maybe mess up your thinking clear about other things.

Viola was finally getting what she wanted in life and there was no power on earth — not the Jabberwock or anything else — that could deny her what she had coming to her.

And maybe … just maybe, there was a whole lot more out there for her to want than she'd known existed and wouldn't that be a hoot. Wouldn't that be a wonder for a fact!

Still, she sat and looked at the house and didn't get out of the car. Smelled the stink of the outhouse out back and the smell so offended her she wanted to hold her nose to make it go away. She'd get used to it in a little bit and wouldn't be able to smell it at all. But now …

There was them little candles in the shiny white bathroom in her new house and even if there was a stink — which there wasn't — them candles filled the room with smells that made you smile just to breathe them.

Seeing her own house every day of her life had made it invisible. You seen a thing day in and day out for going on seven decades and after a while you didn't really see it at all anymore. She was seeing it now, though. Seeing what was there and seeing all that wasn't visible but was as much a part of that house as the shingles on the roof.

Because of what was on her mind, her thoughts went to her babies, the ones buried underneath crosses in the little family cemetery under the cherry tree on the hillside above the house. You couldn't see the cemetery from here, but it was part of what Viola seen when she looked at the house whether her eyes could actually pick it out or not.

She'd lost three children. That wasn't counting the twins the devil took. Elizabeth May had died of pneumonia and Josiah had just … *died.* She went in to nurse him one morning and Joe was lying there cold as a doll in his crib. Ezekiel was almost three when he come down with that influenza thing, throwin' up and diarrhea. Didn't take but two days to kill him. She had put all them little ones in the ground, knew after she birthed Malachi that he was the last, that she wasn't going to be having no more babies. Wasn't no telling what them others woulda grown up to be if they'd had a chance, but it was only Malachi that'd turned out to be worth anything. And he wasn't just the pick of the litter, he was a mother's fantasy of a son — even if he wouldn't do what he was told. He was everything any mother could want, and right now her mind had walled off consideration of what was gonna happen if she found out he'd crossed her. Right now her mind was considering who he was.

And what *else* he might be.

She got out of the car then.

"You wait here. Won't take me long."

She had sent the boys out to collect a few things for her that she needed in her new home. Wasn't but a few things, though. Mostly personal things like clothes, shoes, her hairbrush and the like. Beyond that there wasn't a thing in the whole house that mattered a hill of beans to Viola. Wasn't a thing good and fine and fair to look at like every piece of furniture and picture and gilded mirror and doodad sitting on the tables in her new house.

She never even thought about it as the Nower House no more. It was the Tackett House, would be the Tackett House until her dying breath, and she sure as Jackson didn't intend to clutter it up with worthless things from this place where decades of living had soaked into the walls like sweat into an unwashed work shirt.

What she was looking for was on the top shelf of the chifforobe in her bedroom, way back in the back. She couldn't reach it, but didn't call Zach in to help 'cause this was private business and he wasn't no part of it. She dragged a chair out of the kitchen into the bedroom and put it in front of the big, ugly piece of furniture, climbed up on it, shoved worn quilts and threadbare towels off onto the floor and felt around, located the box there in the back and hauled it down. She carried it into the kitchen and turned it upside down and dumped out the contents on the table.

Wasn't much there. Viola never had been one to hold onto things and she hadn't lived the kind of life where there was much in it you wanted to save. There was a handful of crayon drawings that one or the other of them had done when they was little — she didn't know who had done which but wasn't a one of them that you could figure out what they'd been drawing. Sure wasn't no saved-up report cards. She almost laughed. Like she was proud of how well her kids done in school!

There was Malachi's diploma, though. He'd graduated — disobeying her like he done his whole life, stayed in school when she needed his help with her dope business. And there was some things that'd come in the mail when he was in the military, certificates and citations and the like. After awhile they stopped coming, though, and she figured he hadn't stopped getting such, had just changed his home address so they didn't get sent "home" to his mother.

Near the bottom of the heap were photographs. They had a camera — wasn't a good one. Most of the pictures from it was too dark or blurry, and Viola wouldn't spend money she didn't have on film. She didn't care about such things anyway, but there'd been that time that Obie'd got a burr up his butt to take pictures and he'd gone around taking snapshots of everything he could find until he shot up the whole roll of film. It was probably six or seven months later before he talked her into paying to have the film developed and she remembered how thrilled he'd been when she come home with the envelope of the photographs from the drugstore.

The whole family'd gathered around, wanted to see — at least they did until they saw what he'd took pictures of. A blurry picture of Neb chopping wood, a picture of Viola's back while she washed dishes — things like that. Three or four pictures of the piglets in the barn that was so dark they was just outlines. The only memorable shot was when Obie'd yanked open the privy door and took a picture of Zach doing his business. Everybody got a kick out of that one.

Even it was too dark, though. Something with the camera.

But it wasn't the only memorable shot, because there was another one that had caught Viola's eye at the time, and had hung on a nail in her head all these years. She dug around through the pile, looking for it, sure she hadn't imagined it, hoping it hadn't got lost or accidentally thrown away.

Then she found it.

She held it way out in front of her — away from her face 'cause she had trouble focusing on things close up.

She felt a chill down her spine, like there was an ice cube on the back of her neck and it was melting, icy water that dripped off one bone to the next and to the next, all the way down.

It was a picture of Malachi asleep, not yet a teenager, still a little boy. Between childhood and being a grown man, Malachi's face had changed much more than his brothers' had. Maybe it was just the looks on their faces — like they wasn't a whole lot smarter as grownups than they'd been as kids. But it was really more than that, Malachi's face had become lean, gaunt. His brothers' pudgy faces had not matured like his had.

But in the picture, Malachi's face still bore the soft lines of childhood. He was lying on his right side, had scooted the pillow off onto the floor like he always done so his cheek was resting on the mattress. Wasn't no bottom sheet

— sometimes they was sheets enough to put on all the beds and sometimes not.

Maybe he was sick or taking a nap or something because it wasn't night. Afternoon, though, because there was long shadows everywhere. And the camera'd made the picture too dark just like it'd done all the others, so you couldn't make out much of nothing near the edges.

Musta been right before the sun dropped down below the top of Gizzard Ridge because it sent a last ray of sunlight, a sunbeam like an arrow through the trees and through the window to light up a small portion of Malachi's bedroom. His bed, and his face against the mattress.

Just his face — nothing else, the rest of the room lay in shadows. Far as Viola could remember, only this picture and the one of Zach taking a dump were crisply focused without no blur whatsoever.

His eyes was closed, eyelashes so long you could see 'em on his cheeks, hair all tousled across his forehead. The lines and planes of his face were clear, seemed to pop out in relief against the shadows around him.

A photograph of a sleeping twelve-year-old boy.

Change Malachi's black hair to reddish brown, and this could have been a picture of Rusty Sheridan — who was twelve years old.

The two faces was as alike as brothers.

Or as father and son.

Chapter Nineteen

CHARLIE AND FISH leaned against the wall in the basement of the Methodist church. Charlie had coaxed Fish off the piano stool and sat him down on the floor, there was no other furniture, and then she'd sat down beside him.

Merrie was having a grand time playing with — *destroying* the hundreds of tattered, water-stained hymnals that'd been stacked against the wall. Charlie would buy new ones if there was ever again a congregation here who needed them. The little girl had made paper airplanes and balls out of the pages, had stacked the books up as building blocks for her castle, had torn pages into tiny pieces and made it snow on her castle, and had begged to be allowed to use a pair of Fish's socks — they were clean, hung on the line to dry after he'd washed them — to make sock puppets. Currently, the puppets were castle guards, sticking out over the top wall of the structure and dropping the rocks Merrie'd retrieved from the gravel parking lot onto the heads of an invading army of "dragons" fashioned from balls of paper held together with strips of the tape she'd found in the back of a desk drawer in one of the church offices. Charlie had taken the child on a quick search-and-retrieve mission into the abandoned church office area of the building — avoiding the sanctuary where there was broken glass. Merrie had searched the offices and had returned with all manner of useless flotsam and jetsam to occupy her time.

An incredibly creative child, Charlie thought, watching her play. That little girl could grow up to be — well, anything she wanted … if she got a chance to grow up at all.

Even though Fish was sober, actually appeared to be totally sober, for the first time in who knew how long, he still was far from lucid. Maybe it was alcohol poisoning, all those brain cells that died from being soaked in alcohol for years. Perhaps it was the lingering effects of the DTs — he'd briefly described what he'd suffered after he poured all his booze down the drain. It was horrifying even though she was sure he had sugarcoated reality.

He looked like he'd aged ten years … and smelled like he'd spent the whole decade in the clothes he was currently wearing. He might even have been aware he had a … hygiene problem, because he mentioned that he'd washed all his clothes and hung them on the line so he'd have something clean to wear. Unfortunately for Charlie's olfactory nerves, the clothing was still too wet to change into.

He vacillated between being tense and jittery, his eyes darting from side to side, paranoid that something — likely the Jabberwock, but they hadn't yet gotten too deep into that part of the story — would come for him. Other times, he broke out sobbing for what appeared to be no reason, at least nothing Charlie could tie to the subjects they we're talking about. His emotions didn't fit the circumstances, and his answers to her questions about the Jabberwock were evasive. Clearly, he didn't want to talk about it, but he'd been awake and aware enough this morning to try to order his life, clean up his act, and that intention appeared to be clearing his thinking.

Charlie had done a lot of the talking — to give him time to grab hold of himself after his crying jag. She'd told him about the conversation she, Sam and Malachi had had with Thelma Jackson. How Thelma had told them the Witch of Gideon's daughter said her mother had called the "thing" that had made the town disappear "the Jabberwock."

"She said that was its name," Charlie said. "That it *told her* that was its name."

Fish had dropped his gaze into his lap when she said the word and wouldn't look at her.

"So how did *you* know its name on J-Day?"

Fish wouldn't raise his eyes.

"We all thought you just pulled the verse from the poem out of your cluttered literary mind. But that's not it, is it, Fish?"

He shook his head slowly.

Suddenly, Charlie felt a flash of anger at the dirty old man seated beside her. She didn't have time to play word games here. People were dying.

"Come on, spill it." Her voice had an edge to it now. "You have to tell me whatever you know about the Jabberwock. What do you mean 'you didn't know it could kill people?' What are you talking about?" As an afterthought, she tossed in: "Tell me what you know or you'll have more innocent blood on your hands."

That did the trick, built a fire under the man. He looked up, grabbed her gaze with his bloodshot eyes and said, "I was in Fearsome Hollow. I ... encountered the thing. But I thought at the time it was a fantasy, a hallucination." He averted his eyes momentarily. "That I had fried my mind with too many hallucinogenic drugs so I'd conjured it up in my head."

He stopped.

"I clung to that explanation … that self-delusion for years. Because to believe the thing was real was to … I couldn't believe what I had seen was reality. If I had, I … would have lost my mind."

"So, instead, you tried to erase what you'd seen by soaking it in booze."

"I went back to my house, drove my car, actually got in my car and drove away like the world was a normal place and not a country peopled with monsters with sharp teeth. I went into my kitchen, dug out a bottle of whiskey I'd gotten at the Kentucky Education Association Christmas party in Louisville the year before, and … I think I drank the whole bottle that night." He paused. "I don't believe I have drawn a completely sober breath since that day."

"What did you see in Fearsome Hollow?"

He drew a breath and his voice was soft. "I saw it, the Jabberwock. Only the Jabberwock is not *it*. The Jabberwock is *them*. It's plural. Though perhaps that's not entirely accurate. They function as one entity, so it's a matter of grammatical dispute."

They.

Duh. Of course. When she and Malachi and the Tungates went to Fearsome Hollow looking for Abner that day, there had been more than one thing swirling around the car in the mist. When she and Sam and Malachi were first-graders lost in the mist, they heard voice-*s*, more than one.

"What did it … they … the Jabberwock do?"

"It killed Jamie Forrester. Or not. Maybe not."

"Who is Jamie Forrester?"

"A young man I picked up hitchhiking on Interstate 75.

He said he was bumming his way across the country and when he saw the sign that said, 'Kingdom Come Parkway,' he had to see where *that* led."

A smile tried to flitter across Fish's lips but couldn't make it.

"He was a positively delightful young man — an aspiring Shakespearean actor who loved Keats and Shelley and Burns. A kindred spirit. A soulmate. The boy was terribly disappointed when I told him that the Kingdom Come Parkway was a road *from* nowhere, *to* nowhere, *through* nowhere. So I offered to take him to the closest thing we had to Kingdom Come — a genuine ghost town. I shared with him my cache of goodies." He lifted an eyebrow. "Mild-mannered English teacher by day, psyched out druggie by night."

"So the two of you—?"

"I took him to Gideon. He dropped acid. But before I had a chance to join him in psychedelic lunacy, the *real* monsters showed up."

Chapter Twenty

DRIVING LONG distances were the worst. Hard to distract yourself when you were in a car alone. The radio didn't work and even when it did, Moses could never find anything but country music stations, and crying-in-your-beer songs about trains, dead dogs and unfaithful lovers set Moses's teeth on edge.

Only four and a half, maybe five hours. Two hundred seventy-five miles. That's what he'd figured out pouring over the road atlas, his nose so close to the print on the page he could smell where one of those little barbecue packets burst in his glove box and sprayed the contents as thoroughly as a skunk.

The miles sped past outside his window. The memories came. The groove was deep.

Ghosts lied. Of course they did. People lied and ghosts were people. *Dead* people but people all the same. It was Moses's theory that dying made good people better and bad people worse. It didn't hold true every time, but was accurate more often than not.

And when a person died angry, or afraid, or jealous, or

in a murderous rage ... well, strong emotions like that lingered. Ghosts were no more likely to be benign creatures, devoid of malicious intent, than people were. Moses had run into all kinds since the day more than five decades ago when he briefly visited the land of the dead, when he died, drowned. Then a fireman beat on his back, knocked the water out of his lungs, pounded on his chest until he cracked a rib, but somehow got Moses breathing again. Maybe Moses had left that other world too fast, left the door open a crack and others came through it after him.

He never knew the reason, could only speculate, but after that day, the dead were almost as much a part of his life as the living. They showed up when it suited them, stayed as long as they wanted, and then vanished — literally popped out of existence like a soap bubble — for no reason Moses could understand. Sometimes right in the middle of a sentence.

In the beginning ... well, how many people could see ghosts? Of course, it was entertaining, he made dumb mistakes, told people, got laughed at, had bad encounters. The novelty wore off pretty quickly. Still they were there. Day in, day out. And their presence slowly eroded his soul. Bit by bit, pieces of who he was ... *came loose.* He envisioned it like the pilings of a pier in a storm, the fury of the waves beating against it until it begins to fragment, can't withstand the constant onslaught. It breaks apart, and boards, planking, railing ... it all washes out to sea. The dead people and their horror stories, their unspent emotions, their often evil intent — it chewed away at the man who was Moses Weiss and he had no defense against it.

Nobody but Flossie ever knew the whole extent of it. And after a while, she had to put up a barrier or she'd have gone mad, too. She had to keep him always at arm's length, citing her growing list of mantras like a litany to the Virgin Mary … Say two Hail Marys and two Our Father's …

Brick by brick, she built a wall between them that protected her, that she could hide behind. And he was forever on the other side.

They never made love again after the first year of their marriage. And Moses had remained faithful even then. He didn't blame her, he understood, she should have abandoned him, and in her own way she did, just left her body behind when she bailed out.

Occasionally, his encounters with the dead were somehow beneficial, to them or to the people they'd left behind. It had been that way with Jolene Rutherford and he was sure that was why she'd called him. but it didn't work out that way very often. In fact, the older he got … maybe he just wasn't as resilient as he'd once been. But now, it seemed that every encounter hit a nerve, like cold water on a sensitive tooth. And he was worn out, worn down by it. So very, very tired of formless visages only he could see, dragging him into their dramas and diminishing him by the contact.

He felt … thin.

He suspected that it wouldn't last much longer — that *he* wouldn't last much longer. And maybe that's one reason he had been willing to drop his life and go running off into the mountains of eastern Kentucky to help an old friend — okay, an old acquaintance, because that's really all she was. Maybe that's why he hadn't just called her, asked what her problem was — perhaps he could have helped her with "wise counsel" over the phone.

Of course, that was horse hockey. He'd never helped anybody over the phone, and as soon as he'd heard the desperation in her voice, he'd felt a sense of inevitability settle over him. It would be what it would be. This was a thing he had to do. The next thing. Just do the next thing, that was all anybody could do. And maybe it would be the last thing. Everybody had a last thing and maybe this was his. Maybe this was the last such encounter, *mission* of his life, one he would perform with his last breath.

And that was just fine with Moses Habakuk Weiss. He was bone weary and the prospect of "going out with a bang" had a certain appeal. He'd take that and a twenty and give you back nineteen dollars, ninety-five cents in change.

Chapter Twenty-One

Holmes Fischer and Jamie Forrester sit side by side on the top step of the porch of an abandoned building as the sun sinks down behind Buzzard Knob and its shadow stretches out to claim Fearsome Hollow.

As Jamie rolls two fat joints from the baggie full of weed Fish carries in his glove box, Fish answers Jamie's question about the huge tree in the middle of the street. Fish tells him it's called the Carthage Oak, but he doesn't know where the name came from.

They inhale deeply, enjoying the feel of smoke filling their lungs and the world around them slowly filling with cotton-soft "mellow."

The game of dueling soliloquies begins halfway through the joint.

"But soft, what light through yonder window breaks," Jamie intones, staring glassy-eyed into the trees on the mountains rising up around the town. The boy's words ring true, real, not like some fool making fun of the beauty of the language.

"It is the East, and Juliet is the sun," Fish says, and Jamie looks at him and grins in delight, then finishes the line.

"Arise, fair sun, and kill the envious moon who is already sick and pale with grief."

They move from Romeo and Juliet to Othello.

"I loved Ophelia," Fish begins.

"Forty thousand brothers could not with all their quantity of love make up my sum," Jamie continues.

As the game continues, they finish the joints and Fish pulls out his cache of wonder pills. He had first taken psychedelic drugs when he was in college in the 60's, carried his desire for them and his supply of them into two previous teaching positions before he settled in sleepy Nower County, Kentucky.

Jamie pretends that he is an old hand at dropping acid, but Fish can see it's all a bluff, that the boy is about to take his first trip on the Good Ship Lollipop.

Jamie places a pill on his tongue and dry-swallows, then moves on from Othello to Hamlet. Not the cerebral to-be-or-not-to-be Hamlet, but the man in emotional torment.

"O that this too, too solid flesh would melt, thaw, and resolve itself into a dew ..."

"Or that the Everlasting had not fixed his canon against self-slaughter," Fish continues, unaware at the time that the words would come back to haunt him, to stay his hand when he, like Hamlet, comes to see "how weary, stale, flat and unprofitable seem to me all the uses of this world!"

Fish wants to be sure the boy's ride is a smooth one, so he waits. As soon as he sees the boy's eyes slip out of focus, can tell that what Jamie is looking at does not exist in the natural world around him, Fish prepares to join him. That's when it occurs to Fish that the most right and proper images for their journey come more from Lewis Carroll than Shakespeare.

He stands and calls out in a loud voice the opening line from "Jabberwocky," the nonsense poem from Carroll's Through the Looking-Glass *fantasy.*

"T'was brillig, and the slithy toves did gyre and gimble in the wabe. All mimsy were the borogoves and the more raths outgrabe."

As soon as the words leave his mouth, he feels a chill, as if a breeze off a glacier has lifted the hair off the back of his neck.

He waits for the boy to join in, but it is clear from the vacant look on his face that Jamie Forrester has left the building.

"Beware the Jabberwock, my son!" Fish continues for him. "The jaws that bite, the claws that catch!"

The air thrums violently in Fish's ears. Pressure like dropping in an elevator. The sensation is so violent that he loses his place, forgets the next few lines. His tongue stumbles over the words and he takes up at the next line he remembers.

"… the Jabberwock, with eyes of flame came whiffling through the tulgey wood and burbled as it came."

He is suddenly struck with the sense that some terror, some unnamable horror is lurking out in the shadows just beyond the edges of his vision. And he is only high. Has indulged in nothing more potent than a little weed. Still the sensation is so intense, so visceral, he sucks in a gasp and looks around.

Nothing.

Burping out a self-conscious laugh, Fish lifts his hand to drop the pill on his tongue and proclaims in a firm voice:

"One, two! One, two! And through and through, the vorpal blade went snicker-snack. He left it dead, and with its head, he went galumphing back."

Piercing, wailing shrieks from voices all around him suddenly rip into his ears, the ferocious wave of sound literally dropping him to his knees. How — the acid pill falls out of his suddenly limp fingers to the wooden porch and he watches it roll away — he didn't take it. How—?

Then he lifts his eyes and monsters with eyes of flame come rushing at him out of the surrounding trees.

Inhuman faces distorted by unhinged jaws with impossibly large curved teeth as sharp as razors.

Snarling, snapping teeth. Distorted bodies, deformed … flesh dangling off skeletons in great tatters.

Herky-jerky movements, bloated bellies, surging forward on limbs with bones as thin and fragile as a baby bird's wings.

One.

Five.

A dozen of them.

No, more than that.

Each unique, different in its horror from the next. All in a fury beyond the capacity of human anger.

But they are human.

Were human.

Voices shrieking with such an agony of pain and despair and rage that Fish reaches up to feel blood dripping from his ears.

He staggers to his feet to run. Where? There is no escape from monsters from Hell. And they are all around him.

Jamie stands oblivious to the horror, a lopsided grin on his face.

The first of the monsters leaps up onto the porch, reaches out a witch's hand that ends in claws. The creature rakes them across Jamie's face, opening up gashes to the bone, the white of forehead and cheekbones visible before the gush of blood.

Jamie shrieks.

Fish is too stoned to move effectively, can't coordinate his limbs, staggers as a creature leaps toward him. It's smaller than the one that ripped Jamie's face off, but when it strikes Fish in the chest, it knocks him off balance. He reaches out, arms flailing and strikes Jamie in the back of the head. The young man staggers forward and falls head-first down the steps.

The creature is in Fish's face, gaping maw open to rip out his jugular.

FISH WAS BREATHING in great heaving gasps. Charlie was grateful that his words exploded out of his throat in a strangled whisper Merrie could not hear, tucked away on the other side of the room inside her hymnal castle, singing happily some nonsense song about a witch, a dragon and a doughnut.

She was looking at Merrie when Fish spoke in a normal voice again, not a whisper, though the voice was hoarse.

"It was real." All emotion was seined out of the words. "What I saw was not a drug-induced hallucination. It — they screamed pieces of the poem. 'Jabberwock. Jabberwock. Jabberwock,' the words came from all of them in different voices. The thing, the one, the smaller one that … I could smell its breath like a rotted corpse."

Fish reached up with trembling fingers and began to unbutton his shirt, when he was halfway down, he pulled it open, like Superman displaying the S of his Superman suit on his chest.

Fish wasn't wearing a Superman suit. What he revealed was a bony chest, thin and hairless, with four thick white scars that started low on his right side and swept across his chest and onto his shoulder."

Charlie couldn't help gasping.

Fish slumped back against the wall then, buttoning his shirt.

"I don't know why I didn't die. I thought I had, thought I was dead and had gone to hell. Then I opened my eyes and I was lying on the porch of that building on my back in a puddle of blood, my chest ripped open. And when I got to my knees, I saw Jamie lying in the street below."

He took a shaky breath.

"He was dead. I'm not sure what … how he died, the cause of death. His face was sliced … almost off the front of his head, but I don't think that killed him. I think his neck was broken … which would mean, of course, that *I* killed him. I'm not sure exactly what happened." He paused. "I am making a bit of a habit of that — I don't know what happened to Martha Whittiker, either. But the salient point to remember in both cases is that they ended up dead and it's my fault. I put Martha Whittiker's body in her grandson's apartment, and I threw Jamie Forrester's body down an old well shaft — no one ever knew he was here, that he died here. If he had family — he didn't say — they never knew what happened to him."

Fish barked out a sad laugh into the stunned silence that followed that remark.

"But, of course, I didn't need somebody else to blame me. I blamed myself quite adequately, thank you very much. I tried to punish myself by drinking myself to death. Unfortunately, I survived long enough to kill two more innocent people."

His chin dropped to his chest and he began to cry again.

Chapter Twenty-Two

NEB YELLED AT ESSIE.

"Stop it! Stop that bleedin', you hear me. Stop it right now."

Essie just looked up at him with confused eyes as blood flowed out beneath her in an ever-widening circle on the porch.

What should he do?

What?

Neb was paralyzed, couldn't move even a finger. Locked down like that Tin Man in the Wizard of Oz before Dorothy squirted oil on his joints from the can. The Wizard of Oz was Neb's favorite movie.

His mind bounced off the images of Munchkins and flying witch creatures that didn't have no names and ruby slippers to the pistol lying in the grass. The Smith & Wesson he'd shot his sister with.

Neb quit yelling at her to stop bleeding and just stared at her belly in fascinated horror. He was so scared his bladder let go and he felt warmth between his legs. He'd pissed himself.

Call 911. Yeah, that was it. You was supposed—

Wasn't no 911.

Go for help. Help where?

Wasn't no help anywhere in town. Onliest doctor was a vet and he'd got dog bit and was dying his own self of rabies.

Stop the bleeding. That was the most important thing. Had to stop the bleeding.

Neb accidentally did the next thing right.

He ripped off his tee shirt and wadded it up in a ball and jammed it down on the bloody hole in Essie's tee-shirt, looked around for some way to hold it there.

His fingers shaking, wet and sticky with blood, he ripped off the gun belt, yanked the holsters off it and threw them into the yard and then wrapped the belt around Essie. He lifted her fat body up and scooted the belt under her and then fastened it tight across the wadded-up tee shirt on her belly.

Oh God, oh God, oh God, please don't let her die.

"Don't you die on me," he cried into her face. She didn't look surprised anymore. Her eyes looked dull.

"Heeellllp!" he cried out at the top of his lungs in fear and longing.

Wasn't nobody around to hear him. The Nower House — the *Tackett* House, he'd get in trouble if he didn't call it that — didn't have no close-by neighbors. All the yards on this side of the street were huge, this one in particular, wide areas of grass in front and back. Obie'd left the mower sitting because Neb'd been supposed to finish up mowing the yard only he'd gone in the house instead and got his guns so he could practice—

He'd shot her. Hadn't meant to. It was an accident. He never dreamed the trigger pull on that pistol would be so light he'd pull it just drawing the gun out of the holster.

He hadn't intended for nothing as awful as shooting his sister to happen just 'cause he was playing with them guns.

Only then did the realization strike him — what was Mama gonna do to him when she found out what he'd done?

Found out he'd been playing quick-draw like some little kid and shot ...

What if Essie died? What if he'd ... *killed* her?

No! No, no, no, no. He had to help her, had to keep her from dying, had to do something. He couldn't even load her up and take her ... take her somewhere. He didn't have no car. Obie'd took his pickup to the sheriff's office and Mama'd gone off with Zach in his fancy ...

The truck was out back! The farm truck they'd come to town in. Mama'd lost their pickup truck to the Jabberwock and they'd been driving around in that old truck ever since — 'til Zach and Obie got their own cars. He could load Essie up in the truck and take her ... where?

Where?

To the clinic in the Middle of Nowhere. That's where Sam Sheridan was!

Yeah. He'd take Essie there and Sam could fix her up, make her good as new like she'd done when that spider had bit him. Hadn't nothing in Neb's life hurt like that did, and then it'd got infected. He started running a fever, sick like he had the flu and Mama'd sent Obie down to ask Eunice Martin would she please call Sam Sheridan and ask her to come by and see to him.

By the time Sam got there, Neb was so sick he barely knew what was going on, just remembered Sam had jumped dead in the middle of Mama for not calling her sooner, said that infected bite coulda killed Neb! Mama took Sam's yellin' meek as a lamb.

Yeah! Neb had to load Essie up in that old truck and take her to Sam at the clinic.

How was he gonna get her to the truck?

He'd have to carry her. But Essie was almost big as he was. And Neb wasn't strong like his brothers. How was he supposed to pick up big ole Essie and carry her all the way around the house to the truck?

Essie made a little moaning sound, pitiful-like, sounded like a baby rabbit the dogs had got to and 'fore Neb knew it he had reached down and lifted her up into his arms and was staggering down the porch steps with her.

Wasn't no way he coulda done it if he'd thought about it but he didn't think, just done it. Stumbled to his knees and very near dumped her in the grass at the bottom of the porch steps, but he made it back up to his feet and lurched across the yard toward the driveway that led to the garages in the back of the house. Three of 'em. A double garage on one side and then a single one alongside it, but the single one was filled up with junk Mama hadn't yet decided what to do with — stuff belonging to the Nower family that Sebastian hadn't took with him when she run him off.

The farm truck was parked in front of the single garage. Neb gasped for breath, stumbled toward it, had made it halfway down the driveway when he heard a sound from the street and cried out his own self in relief, then dropped to his knees. The vroom-vroom sound purred softer as Zach pulled his fancy black sports car into the driveway, taking the corner too fast so the tires squealed when he stopped. Neb laid Essie down on the concrete and leapt up, went running to his mother who was climbing out of the car.

Neb was crying, blubbering, snot running down his lip, babbling.

"Mama, Mama, Essie's hurt."

Mama could see that her own self soon's she got out of the car and she run up the driveway and knelt beside where he'd left Essie. Mama let out a little cry of surprise and put her hands on Essie's cheeks, patting them.

"I's trying to get her to the truck so's I could take her to Sam out in the Middle—

"What happened?" Mama fired the words into the air. "She fall down, hurt herself …?"

Mama was examining the wad of his tee-shirt strapped to Essie's belly with his belt.

"She didn't fall, Mama. She … been shot."

Mama's head snapped toward him and her eyes bored into him like railroad spikes.

"Shot? Essie, shot?" Surprise and shock were instantly replaced by anger. "Who done it? Who shot my Essie?"

"I don't know, Mama," Neb heard his mouth say. "I didn't see who done it. I was … mowing the lawn, just like you said, and I heard a bang, and I come running 'round the side of the house as a car was driving away. Found Essie on the porch. Shot."

It hadn't occurred to Neb until that moment to lie, and he'd said the first thing that come to mind. But it was a good story. Somebody drove by the house and shot Essie. And he never seen who it was.

The story worked. Neb didn't have no gun on him. He'd dropped both the pistols in grass so tall you'd have to step on 'em to see 'em, the holsters, too, even took off the gun belt and used it to hold Essie's bandage in place.

Of course, Essie knew what really happened, but she couldn't talk clear enough to make much sense out of her words. Couldn't hardly understand nothing she said.

The flame of pure hatred and rage in Neb's mother's eyes was a horror to behold as she looked out at the street, considering the imaginary gunman who'd shot down her baby girl. Then she banked the fire, left the heat of it bright behind her eyes as she focused on Essie.

"Zach, get in the house and call Obie and tell him to get here fast in his truck."

Obie. Neb hadn't even thought to call Obie.

Then his mama took Essie's hand and patted it, told her she was gonna be just fine, petted her cheek and stroked her forehead, running her hand back over Essie's mostly bald head.

It occurred to Neb only then how enormous it was that he'd dodged the bullet of responsibility for what had happened to his sister. He surely wouldn't want to be the one who eventually caught the blame for the deed. He literally couldn't imagine what his mother was gonna do to whoever she held to account for it.

Chapter Twenty-Three

MALACHI FACED the deranged father of a dead teenager —
the grandfather of the baby she carried — and knew it
would do no good to argue with him. Duncan Norman
was way past the ability to reason. Nothing Malachi said
would convince him that Malachi had not ... what was it
he was babbling, *ravished* his precious baby girl. From the
little pieces of coherent thought in the reverend's ravings
Malachi pieced together that he knew the father of Haley's
baby was Malachi because he had read it in her diary.
Which made no sense at all. Malachi knew the teenager, of
course, at least knew who she was, remembered her from J-
Day, sitting blinded in the parking lot in the Middle of
Nowhere, asking where her vehicle was, refusing to tell Fish
where she'd been going.

Sam said Hayley'd told her she'd been on her way to
Lexington that day to get an abortion. And when she
couldn't get one, and Sam refused to perform one, the
baby's father, *Howie Witherspoon*, had killed her.

But there was no way now to get Duncan Norman to
believe that, no way was he rational enough to compre-

hend it. Malachi had to get the gun away from him. He doubted Norman's reflexes were quick enough to fire before Malachi jumped him. He hoped they weren't — his life depended on that. But he needed a second, just a moment, had to catch the man off guard.

And then Malachi noticed the bloody handprint on the window.

"I'm not your man," Malachi said. "And I can prove it."

"Don't you even have the decency to admit what you did?"

"Look at the car window, Duncan."

"The window *you* smeared with my daughter's blood!"

"The handprint, Duncan. Look at the handprint!"

He saw Duncan cut his eyes toward the window only for an instant but long enough to see the print on the glass. It looked like somebody had stuck their hand down into a can of red paint and then carefully applied it to the window pane. Not just somebody, of course. Howie Witherspoon.

"The person who killed your daughter came back to her car after he committed the crime," Malachi was careful not to say words that would incite him. Left out "beat your daughter until she was unrecognizable" and "threw her dead body off the cliff."

"Shut up. Just shut your filthy mouth." Duncan seemed to grab hold of the impending explosion of rage then. Took a breath. "You have until I count to ten to make your peace with God. A man like you doesn't even believe there is a God but the second I put a bullet through your heart, you will discover how very wrong you are. There is a God and there is a devil. You and Satan are about to become besties."

He paused.

"One."

"The man who killed your daughter had her blood on his hands and he smeared it on the car. You can see that."

"Two."

"He placed his hand on the front window to close the front door."

"Three."

"He left a bloody handprint there."

"Four."

Malachi had to take a chance. He reached out slowly toward the mark on the window.

"I told you not to move."

"The handprint, Duncan. The man who killed your daughter made it with her blood. *Look at it.*"

Duncan did glance at it then, but only glanced. Not good enough.

"And you know that because it was *you* who made the hand print."

"No, it *wasn't* me. And I can prove it — that is *not* my handprint." Duncan kept his eyes trained on Malachi, but surely he could see the handprint out his peripheral vision.

"I am going to open this car door. If you have to shoot me, shoot me. And then after I'm dead you will see that I couldn't have been the man who killed your daughter."

Duncan didn't move, stood frozen.

Malachi moved his hand slowly to the door handle, pulled on it, and eased the door open. Then he pointed to the handprint.

"This is the handprint of the man who killed your daughter. And it is *not* mine."

Malachi put his own hand up to the glass on the inside, in the spot where there was a bloody handprint on the outside. Malachi's right hand lined up perfectly with the bloody left-hand print on the other side of the glass and it was instantly clear what he meant. Malachi had big hands. His sergeant had called them catcher's-mitt hands. Apparently, Howie Witherspoon'd had very small hands, but his fingers were pudgy, like sausages. The bloody handprint was clearly, noticeably *smaller* than Malachi's hand. Malachi's fingers were thinner than the handprint, too, but at least half an inch longer. The handprint's palm was rounded, Malachi's was thin and angular and much bigger.

"That's not my handprint, couldn't be. You can see that. I didn't kill your daughter."

Malachi tensed to jump.

Chapter Twenty-Four

"My fraternity brothers always said that the reason beer went through your system so fast was because it didn't have to pause inside to change colors before you peed," Stuart said. "So I don't get why this coffee is draining through me like there's a hose connecting one end to the other. Coffee *does* have to pause inside to change colors."

Filters were definitely going down. With all three of them sleep-deprived, there was no telling what might come out of their mouths. Cotton suspected Stuart McClintock wouldn't likely have dropped that comment into polite conversation if he weren't bleary-eyed with exhaustion.

But Cotton had to keep shoving coffee down Stuart's throat because the man refused to take the NoDoz tablets Cotton had bought. And Stuart had to stay awake — they all did. Could not go to sleep. Cotton thought of the dark areas outside the known world on ancient maps that bore the notation "Beyond Here Be Dragons."

Sleep was now a dark void beyond the boundaries of awareness — a land of dragons. And worse.

There was a knock at the kitchen door. He and Stuart

turned from their coffee and looked through the curtained window to see a man standing on the back porch. Stuart shot Cotton a questioning look and Cotton shrugged. He had no idea who the man was.

When Cotton opened the door, the man took off his rain hat — it wasn't raining, but he was dressed in a raincoat — and introduced himself.

"My name is Moses Weiss," he said. "Are you Cotton Jackson? I do surely hope so. These roads … and the map doesn't … and when I stopped to ask …"

"Nobody was home," Stuart said from behind Cotton.

"Precisely," the man said. "I'm looking for Jolene—"

"Moses!" Jolene cried from the doorway into the hall. She hurried to the door as best she could, favoring her injured arm, to greet the old man. She started to hug him, but didn't, seemed to think better of it.

"Please come in, Mr. Weiss," Cotton said with as much of a flourish as he could muster.

"Oh, no, no, no, not Mr. Weiss. Oh dear no, call me Moses, please. I'm just plain Moses."

Cotton nodded. "The house isn't much … now. But I call it home." To Stuart, he said, "Would you go get one of those folding stools from the camping gear?"

The old man stepped through the doorway, then stepped back out onto the porch. He repeated the procedure twice, saw the curious looks and said simply.

"I am a prisoner of my proclivities, I'm afraid. As I get older, I am less vigilant, and they have gained substantial ground. Too much effort to resist. Too much."

Stuart returned with the folding stool, placed it at the table and sat in it himself, offering one of the three real chairs to the old man. As Moses took off the useless raincoat and hat and handed them to Cotton, Jolene bubbled with gratitude for him "coming all this way" in response to her call.

The man was small and stooped, his shoulders rounded. His white hair was thin and wispy and when he took off his hat, the static electricity made what little there was stand out in a halo around his head. He was wearing a leather apron under the raincoat. Odd. Like he'd leapt up from whatever he was doing — Jolene said he was a cobbler — and run out the door. After a few minutes in the old man's presence, it wasn't at all hard to imagine the old man doing just that. Cotton offered him coffee and he declined, for which Cotton was grateful because he only had the three mugs and he'd hate to have to wash one of them out for the guest.

Moses brushed off Jolene's babbled gratitude and greetings, just sat in the offered chair across from Stuart and pointed to the bandage on Jolene's shoulder.

"Cut yourself, did you?"

For an old man, his voice was strong and he spoke loud. Maybe that was because he was hard of hearing.

She looked to Stuart, who looked to Cotton, who handed the ball right back to Jolene. Let her decide what to tell the old man.

"Not a cut," she said. "A gunshot wound."

The old man didn't blink. "Yes, just so."

"I don't think that's the place to start, though, Moses," she said, gently easing herself down into a chair. "It's kind of a … I don't know, a side issue. The important thing, the reason I called is—"

"Real ghosts, you said. If you don't mind my saying, that's quite a claim coming from you." Before she could protest, he held up his hand. "I believe you, you know. What is it they say — even a blind squirrel gets a nut now and then. It was bound to happen. You shook so very many trees, my dear, you were bound to get hit with an acorn eventually."

"That's not how it happened, Moses. I didn't come here looking for … spirits. I came looking for my father."

And then they told him the story, condensing it as best they could, but it was quite a tale to tell and each of them contributed their parts.

The man asked no questions as they spoke. The same half smile remained on his lips and he nodded at certain points, looked compassionate or confused or whatever was appropriate at other points. He just soaked it all up with no effort to filter or clarify.

But his hands, his fingers began to … twitch. Not twitch, exactly. It started as a little wiggling motion, like a silly goodbye wave, in the fingers of his right hand. It wasn't long before the other hand took up the motion. Cotton supposed it was an unconscious thing like drumming your fingers on a table because Moses appeared oblivious to the motion. But it was disconcerting to watch and Cotton could tell the other two were having as much trouble not staring at it as he was.

The telling, even as freeze-dried as they could make it, took more than an hour. By the time they were done, Moses had moved his hands together on the table and his fingers' dancing motions were intertwined. Occasionally, he would clasp the fingers on one hand with the fingers on the other — and then his thumbs would spin around and around each other in a remarkable display of thumb twiddling. Then he'd let go and return to the fidgeting/twitching/wiggling/dancing fingers again.

When the three storytellers had finally run out of steam, they fell silent. The old man said nothing. Just kept half-smiling and finger-diddling. Finally, Jolene asked, "Well?"

He shook his head, looked resigned. "I suppose you've asked me here to have a chat with one of the spirits. Yes?"

Jolene looked at the others and they all nodded.

Moses's fingers stilled. He sat motionless for a time that got right up to the edge of uncomfortable and when he finally spoke it was in that loud, commanding voice, but in a tone of resigned sadness. Cotton felt compassion for the old man, though he didn't know what for.

"Contrary to common wisdom, or myth, there aren't ghosts floating around — they don't even 'float,' by the way — everywhere you go. Imagine if every person who has ever died remained present as a spirit on the earth — they'd be jammed together so tight they couldn't move. Only a very, very few spirits remain and those who do stay only for a very short time."

"But what about haunted houses where the ... I don't know — the ghost of Aunt Matilda has been slamming doors and levitating vases for two hundred years?" Stuart asked.

"I'm describing 'usual' and 'ordinary.' There are always exceptions."

"Tell us about the *un*usual, the ... *un*-ordinary ones, then, because what we're dealing with here isn't likely to fit neatly into anybody's definition of the way things normally happen," Stuart said. "The spirits who stay, the few who hang around — what's the reason they don't ... move on. To wherever it is ghosts go."

Stuart sat back suddenly and rolled his eyes.

"Listen to me! I'm sitting here discussing ghosts and hauntings and ... as if they were as real as—"

"They *are* real. The reason you don't know that is because the number of people who are aware of their presence ..." He cast a sideways glance at Jolene. "Who can *really* sense their essence is a number so small ... oh, my … I'm seventy-three years old and I've met only two other people I was sure could see what I can see, and one of those was" — his face looked pained — "insane. Drove him quite mad, you see."

The old man's fingers began to dance again. Cotton thought the action resembled Irish folk dances, where the upper part of the dancers' bodies remained totally immobile as they swayed and clipped and clopped merrily — from the waist down.

"I don't know all the reasons why they stay. It's not like there's some kind of S'posta Book to tell you how things are supposed to operate in the spiritual realm. From my own experience …" He paused and his hand motion changed from dancing fingers to rubbing his hands together as if he were scrubbing them, as Pilot had washed his hands of Jesus's blood. "Sometimes they have left something important unfinished, or they can't find something precious to them, or they were interred in the wrong place or not at all or they died in some … horrific fashion. Sometimes they're in the grip of a strong emotion — anger, fear, grief …"

"You feel what they feel, don't you, Moses?" Jolene said softly.

"Oh my yes, indeed yes. Almost always … though sometimes not. Hard to say anything happens every time because each encounter is unique, as individual as the people, the spirits I meet."

He stopped talking, seemed to become aware of his hands, looked up from them sheepishly and clasped them tightly together on the table in front of him.

"You haven't told me why you want me to talk to these spirits—"

"We want to know what happened!" Stuart interrupted.

"Ask them where they are and who—" Cotton said.

Moses interrupted. "Oh, dear. So sorry. 'Fraid I can't help you with all that."

Cotton and the others were confused.

"It isn't up to me what spirits reveal. I can ask them questions, but often … either they don't hear me or they don't care to answer. It's not like you can get a spirit to do something it doesn't want to do. And sometimes, all I get is —" He stopped and a look of such horror took over his face that Cotton turned to look over his own shoulder, fearing the man was seeing some monstrous thing in the room behind him. "Is what they *feel!*" He shuddered. "Or memories, visions of how they died that …"

He stopped talking abruptly, as if he'd slammed some internal door on his thoughts. The other three didn't know what to say. When the old man began speaking again, he sounded tired, as exhausted as the three of them felt.

"Please … select a … *kind* spirit. I'm a very old man and I should like very much to avoid as much conflict as possible." He looked at Jolene. "How about your father?" He turned to Stuart. "Or we could begin with your wife."

Clearly, the old man wasn't expecting the blowback.

"No, you can't talk to my father! He's not dead!"

"Neither is my wife!"

"Oh, dear, I didn't mean to offend."

"The little girl, Rose Topple, you remember what Cotton told you about her?" Jolene said and the old man nodded. "Her father didn't die … instantly. And we—"

"Oh, I see. How very interesting. So you don't think the people who vanished are *dead.*"

"Some of them are," she said. "Some of them must be. That's who we wanted you—"

"I think we should go to the Potters' house," Cotton said. "It's on Elkhorn Road, right off Danville Pike, only a couple of miles. And you could … talk to Amelia, Selma or Becky Sue. Yesterday afternoon when we came back here, the Potters' house was … it's old now. It was fine when we drove past it on the way to Fearsome Hollow."

Cotton hadn't pointed it out because it had hit him in the gut when he saw the ruin. Becky Sue Potter was pregnant. He'd seen her in Persimmon Ridge a couple of days before J-Day. She'd looked then like she could pop any day and that was more than two weeks ago.

"Then let's go," Stuart said and stood. "Every minute we wait … every minute …" He didn't finish because he didn't have to.

Chapter Twenty-Five

Duncan Norman had intended to shoot Malachi Tackett the instant he pulled the gun out of his pocket, had planned to shoot him down like a dog with no warning. But he found he couldn't do that. As soon as Malachi turned to him, recognized Duncan's intent, Duncan was seized with an overwhelming need to empty his rage out on the man before he killed him. He could not help exploding in a torrent of filthy words he had only heard but never used, never even thought, in his whole life.

But none of the words was vile enough. Nothing he said was hideous enough to convey what he was feeling, to make Malachi Tackett understand the magnitude of the horror he had perpetrated.

Images flashed through his mind as he spoke, of his poor child attacked by this tall, dark man, overpowered and raped. Raped. It was an ugly word but not nearly ugly enough for the deed it described. There was no word ugly enough, but Duncan stood there spewing out obscenities in an effort to find one.

He finally wound down, realized he was babbling,

speaking without any meaning, not even condemning the man because he had ceased to make sense.

He stopped then, took in a deep breath. Since he had not shot Malachi on sight as he intended, he found himself prompted by long experience, by some tiny semblance of the man he once was, the man he had been until he saw the mangled body of his baby girl in the freezer drawer at Bascum's.

She had no face. He had beat her so badly she …

But Duncan was a man of God, *had been* a man of God. He'd spent his whole life in that role and discovered he could not so easily shed it now, not even in such an extreme circumstance. He knew what he must do, what he *had to* do. The *Reverend* Duncan Norman was required by everything he was about to allow this … *monster* to make his peace with God. Not for the sake of Malachi's soul. A man who'd done what he had done had no soul. Not for Malachi's soul, but for his own.

He would give him to the count of ten. Ten seconds, that was all.

When Duncan began to count, Malachi spoke. Duncan found that he could only barely hear the man's words through a great buzzing sound that had started up in his ears. In his head. A dozen cicadas. A hundred. A thousand.

Something about the blood on the car. Hayley's blood, precious Hayley's blood. On the hands of her murderer.

Now his finger began to apply pressure to the trigger and he was having trouble controlling the urge.

To the count of ten. That's what he'd said. He was a man of his word.

Something about the handprint. Duncan wasn't so stupid that he would glance away and give the man a chance to jump him. The man was a trained soldier.

Duncan would not win a fight with him, and he didn't intend to get into one.

Duncan heard Malachi's words through the buzz. He said the bloody handprint on the car window wasn't his.

Duncan paused at that. Just paused.

Then Malachi opened the door and placed his hand on the inside of the window, on the other side of the glass from the bloody shape on the outside of the window.

Malachi's hand was larger than the bloody handprint.

Not just a little bit — way bigger, his fingers maybe an inch longer than the handprint of dried blood.

How could that be?

No.

Duncan shook his head. Backed up from the idea with every fiber of who he was, every molecule of his existence. The idea was too horrible to contemplate. That he'd been *wrong!* No. *No!* He had found the man responsible for his precious baby's death. He *had!* The right man. He hadn't made some horrific mistake. He had found the monster and was about to inflict upon him the wrath of a righteous God. It was not possible that the man before him was not the murderer. Because if Malachi Tackett hadn't killed Hayley, *who* ...?

No.

He felt a mindless black horror well up in his chest, swell inside him, like one of those Navy dinghies when you pull the cord. So hideous — growing bigger and bigger until his soul couldn't contain it and it tore free, gushed out of his innermost being like the putrid pus of a cancerous sore.

Noooo!

It was too horrifying, too—

Something fundamental split apart inside Duncan Norman in that instant. Who he was tore asunder as surely as the veil in the temple had ripped when Christ died. From the bottom to the top, and the veil fell away. When it did, Duncan Norman could *see*.

He could see Malachi Tackett *change*.

As Duncan watched in stupefied horror, Malachi became on the outside the demon he was on the inside. Duncan had heard of such things. He'd seen other Pentecostal ministers expel demons from members of their congregations. Though he'd never personally had such an experience, Duncan did believe people could be possessed.

But this wasn't possession. The man who was Malachi Tackett hadn't been possessed by a demon. There was no man. *Malachi Tackett was a demon.*

God had removed the veil from Duncan Norman's eyes so he could see reality. Before him was a demon, a hideous monster who served the Father of Lies. A devil who knew nothing but trickery and deceit. A creature who had brought with him from the bowels of hell the power to *distort reality* — to change the shape of a smear of blood or the shape of a man's hand.

A demon whose only reason for existence was to "steal, kill and destroy." This creature had raped, had *planted his seed* — the devil's git — inside Duncan's precious daughter. This demon had murdered, *butchered* Hayley and now it would kill Duncan, too. He couldn't stop a demon with a mere bullet. When Duncan squeezed the trigger, the demon would only laugh at him. The monster had been waiting for this moment, eager to see the look on Duncan's face, hungry to gloat on a mere mortal's helplessness. Duncan could empty the gun, fire every one of the bullets in the chamber and they would have no effect. It would take far greater force than a bullet to harm an emissary of Satan.

Duncan's virgin daughter had been raped, impregnated and then *murdered* by a demon. And Duncan was powerless to avenge her death. Now the beast would rise and strike down Duncan, too, beat him until his body was unrecognizable just like Hayley's. And no one would ever know that a demon walked the earth in the form of Malachi Tackett, who would rape and kill at will with nobody to stop him.

Unless …

Duncan's heart had been frozen in his chest but now it rumbled back to life. It hammered, pulsing in the veins of his temples with every beat. Perhaps there *was* a force strong enough …

Could Duncan …?

He could. He *would.* It would be a small price to pay for a full measure of vengeance, retribution and *justice.*

But he would have to trick the devil himself.

Still … the God of the universe was on Duncan's side.

Duncan suddenly drew his hand back and threw the pistol as far as he could across the parking lot. Malachi was between him and a scenic little footpath that meandered through the woods to the overlook, so Duncan took off running toward the trees that stretched out to the cliff that ran the length of the whole north side of Ironwood Mountain. On the other side of those woods, the mountain terminated in a drop-off — jagged and rugged, not as clean a cliff face as the Scott's Ridge Overlook. Duncan had to get there before the demon caught up with him.

He prayed for the help of Almighty God — and ran!

Chapter Twenty-Six

COTTON SAID THE POTTERS' house was only a couple of miles down the road. Jolene didn't know the people and she'd been in no shape last night to notice a new "old house." But when they pulled up in front of the place, she did remember it. It had been a red-brick house, set back from the road beyond a big yard, that had an old-fashioned walking bridge over the creek out front. You didn't see many of those anymore but they used to be standard equipment for houses built on the other side of a creek that could flood in a heartbeat with a spring rain. The bridges were fastened between big trees on either side of the creek banks, and spanned the distance with plank flooring and side railings fashioned out of rope like the fisherman's nets on shrimp boats in the Gulf of Mexico she'd seen when she'd been filming a haunted house in southern Louisiana.

She'd noticed the bridge the first time she passed it, on Sunday, riding with Stuart and Cotton after she'd first met them.

The bridge was nowhere in evidence now when they pulled off Elkhorn Road. The house that set behind the overgrown yard was a dilapidated shack, sagging roof, missing walls.

A wreck that appeared to be a century old.

They got out of Stuart's red Lexus and stood staring at the shack.

"You're saying that yesterday morning this …"

"It was a neat little house with a walking bridge, and now …" Jolene let it go.

"And it's your belief that when these houses age, it's a sign that the people who lived in them have died."

"It's just a guess," Cotton said.

"But the Reece family was definitely dead," Stuart said. "Only they … weren't."

He didn't elaborate. They hadn't told Moses about that particular little foray into Nutcase-ville. If they'd told him everything, all the details, they'd still be sitting in Cotton's kitchen. And now didn't seem the time to bring up the Reece family.

Obviously, Moses didn't pick up on the omission.

He wandered off toward the house, across the dry creek bed, and out over the not-there-anymore lawn. Cotton hurried to join him. Stuart pulled up beside Jolene behind the two of them, maybe so he could be there to grab her if she toppled over, but she wasn't as fragile now as she'd felt before. She had a bad cut on her upper arm — needed stitches but was being held together nicely by the butterfly bandages Cotton'd applied. Once the Oxycontin had worn off, it ached, but at least she was no longer so drugged she couldn't think.

"How'd you meet this guy?" Stuart asked as they picked their way through the weedy expanse of creek bank that bore no resemblance at all anymore to the well-kept lawn it had been only a couple of days ago. Jolene was struck anew by the impossibility of it all. How could a being … any being … How did the Jabberwock control time …

She let it go.

"I met him when we were on a shoot in Nashville. In the ghost-hunting world, word gets around. I'd heard about him and wanted to check him out. He's a cobbler so I broke a buckle on a pair of sandals as an excuse to go to his shop."

She winced but not from the pain in her shoulder. "I'd have been up the creek if he'd been a great ghost hunter but a lousy cobbler because those shoes were expensive — Louboutin red sole ankle-wrap—" She stopped, could see that Stuart wasn't tracking. "Well, your wife would definitely recognize the brand!"

She wanted to yank the words back out of the air as soon as they left her lips. They hit Stuart like a blow to the belly and Jolene hurried on to cover her gaffe.

"But he was excellent at both — fixed my shoes and found my ghost. Well, my sound man's ghost."

Jolene often arranged for locals to work on her tech crew so she didn't have to haul an army along with her to shoots all over the country. The man running sound was a Nashville native, a blond Asian — ah, the surprises of random genetic hookups. He had shown up late for an afternoon shoot because he'd been attending his grandmother's funeral. As the crew sat around eating pizza on their dinner break, the young man told his grandmother's story. The woman'd had more than a few missing nuts and bolts and the family knew she was a hoarder, but they'd been unprepared for a house stacked so full of junk it was only possible to walk through it down aisles between ceiling-high stacks of old newspapers, magazines and who knew what else.

"His grandmother'd had a ring — a family treasure

that *her* grandmother had sewn into the hem of her dress when the family'd fled from the approaching Japanese Army during the Sino-Japanese War a hundred years ago. The family tore the house apart — found a little tin box under a loose floorboard and the contents rattled so they were sure they'd hit pay dirt. Not. The box was filled with his grandmother's old fingernail and toenail clippings."

"She *kept*—?"

Jolene nodded.

"I'd only just met Moses, but he'd seemed legit — by my definition, meaning he wasn't a con. Crazy, maybe, but he genuinely believed he could talk to the dead. So I asked if he'd try to have a chat with the old hoarder."

"And did he?"

Jolene nodded.

"He said she was a charming nutcase, totally dithered, had rambled on about everything and nothing until she happened to mention that she was concerned about someone in the family breaking a tooth. Seems she had stuffed the ring down into three pounds of ground meat and froze it in the freezer."

Stuart was awed. "You're serious, aren't you?"

"As a heart attack. Now, how do you explain away something like that? How could he possibly have known unless …? He's the only person I ever met I believed really could communicate with ghosts."

Cotton and Moses had reached the house and Stuart nodded at them.

"Let's hope these dead people are the chatty sort."

Chapter Twenty-Seven

WHAT THE ...?

Duncan Norman suddenly threw away the pistol he'd had trained on Malachi, pitched it with all his strength into the parking lot and then turned and ran away toward the woods.

Malachi was so surprised, he froze, then slowly collapsed back onto the side of the car and allowed relief to flood over him in a warm tide.

He'd been mistaken about Duncan Norman. Malachi really hadn't believed he'd be able to convince the man he hadn't killed Hayley. He'd thought Duncan was clinging to his sanity by his fingernails and wouldn't be able to focus on the evidence, the bloody handprint that could not possibly have been Malachi's.

Malachi had been wrong about that.

It took him a few moments to gather himself, come down off the adrenaline high that he recognized so well from combat. When your life was in danger, when you'd selected fight from the fight-or-flight menu offered by your pituitary, the gland dumped adrenaline into your bloodstream. It sharpened your senses — you could see clearer, hear better. It also gave you tunnel vision, so you could focus on whatever was in front of you with more intensity. And the legendary extra strength that gave mothers the power to lift a car off their crushed child — that had saved Malachi's bacon more than once.

He'd have used it to cover the ground between him and Duncan in one leap, had already tensed for the move when Duncan …

Threw the gun away.

The man had finally come to his senses. Malachi shook his head. Having no children of his own, he couldn't relate to the kind of agony it must be to lose one. The agony Charlie had felt when she thought Merrie was locked in an airless kiln. The kind Sam felt right now with Rusty lying unconscious on a bed in the clinic.

And the agony that had driven a Pentecostal minister to get a gun — where had he come by a gun? — and plan to commit murder.

Malachi gave him a little while, then crossed the parking lot and walked into the trees where Duncan had run. The stretch of woods wasn't very wide. On the other side was the spectacular view you could see from the overlook, except the trees blocked it here unless you were standing just out beyond them on the rock ledge. The overlook area had been built on the perfect spot on the mountainside. Below it was a sheer cliff, as smooth and featureless as if it'd been cut with a butter knife, a drop of two hundred feet to the rocks in the Rolling Fork River. On both sides of the overlook cliff face, the mountainside was rugged, lumpy and bumpy with jutting rocks, scraggly bushes poking through cracks, kudzu vines reaching out tendril fingers, clawing for purchase, and piles of boulders at the base.

He spotted Duncan as soon as he entered the woods, standing with his back to Malachi, staring out over Dragonroot Hollow.

"This was Hayley's favorite place in the world," he said when he heard Malachi approaching. "She'd beg me to bring her here when she was a little girl, and came here on her own when she got her driver's license."

He kept talking as Malachi came closer.

"I didn't know that until I read … I wouldn't have intruded on my daughter's privacy except … I found her diary hidden in her room, and I read it. She wrote there about coming here, about how peaceful she felt when she looked out over all that God had created."

Duncan glanced over his shoulder but didn't turn, just kept talking softly. Malachi stepped closer to hear him, pushing a low-hanging tree limb out of the way.

"That's why I thought you …" Duncan took a breath and Malachi could tell he was fighting to keep his voice level. "In her diary, she wrote about what … had happened to her. That she had been … raped."

Hayley Norman hadn't been raped. Obviously, she'd had a longstanding affair with Howie, with Sugar Bear. From what Toby'd said he overheard his father yell at her on the phone that afternoon — "I said not to call me here!" — her calls must have been a frequent occurrence.

Malachi supposed the girl couldn't face reality, so she'd just made something up.

He came to stand beside Duncan, looked out over the vista. Duncan turned to him. "She described in her diary the man who … the man who attacked her. And the description matched … I thought it was you."

He swallowed, his mouth working to keep from crying.

"I'm … sorry, Malachi."

He reached out his hand to shake and Malachi took it.

"It's okay, I—" Malachi began.

Duncan's face suddenly changed. Shamed contrition morphed in a split second into blinding hatred. Triumph blazed in his eyes. His handshake became an iron grip.

Malachi understood then, but it was too late.

With a mighty lunge, Duncan Norman flung himself off the edge of the cliff.

And dragged Malachi Tackett over the edge with him.

Chapter Twenty-Eight

Moses didn't like this. Oh, no he did *not*, no, no, no he did not, *not*. Wanted no part of this, wanted to flee, hide, get as far away as he could. So he turned around in his tracks and took off running.

Except he didn't.

Felt his legs pumping beneath him like he was a young man again — not a skeleton whose knees sounded like popcorn when he knelt down — running fast and free.

But he kept walking.

He was beside the big man whose name was Stuart … something, Moses couldn't remember, never had been good with names even before everything started to go. He looked familiar somehow, like Moses ought to recognize him. An actor. An athlete.

A butcher, a baker, a candlestick maker.

Maybe his face was on some product — breakfast cereal or jockey shorts.

With every step, the light dimmed. Maybe it really did dim, but Moses didn't think so. The light dimmed only in his own consciousness. With every step, he got closer and closer to the cold and dark and—

No, not cold — hot, fiery hot. Rage.

No, cold, frigid and frozen. The heat was behind the cold, hiding there so you didn't even know it was there until it leapt out at you.

Crazy, that was crazy. Nothing was going to leap out at him. Couldn't let his imagination run away with him. Couldn't get dragged out onto the pier in the storm, with the angry waves battering it. The pier was breaking apart, had been for a long time. The boards, the planking, the railing, coming undone. If he were standing on it when … he would wash out to sea with all the shattered pieces.

The house was a shack full of shadows, and more than shadows, dark presences. Oh, this was bad, very bad. The darkness was everywhere around but it was formless and with no shape maybe it was harmless.

Not harmless, definitely not harmless.

It was so cold here, so cold.

Hot, back behind it, all the fires of hell raged.

She was sitting on the floor of the shack. He spotted her the moment he stepped inside. He could barely make out the shapes of furniture around her and she was sitting on a chair or a couch maybe. No, a bed. Where she was, she was on a bed, or thought she was.

She was crying. Heartbroken.

So cold. So hot. Shadows getting darker and darker and darker.

Moses had never encountered anything like this, not ever before. And he wondered if the older you got, the more you could see. That it had been like this all along, with shapes and presences, and emotions and shadows all around, but he just couldn't see them before. And now he could.

No. Nothing had ever been like this.

It was pulsing. A big, black, hateful thing of absolute darkness was throbbing like a heartbeat behind the cold and light. It was angry. Just a tiny whiff of the acrid smell of rage wafted off it, like smelling a single rose in a vase, behind a closed door in a house, when you walked by outside on the sidewalk.

But it burned his nose, just the little whiff.

Never had he dreamed there could be such anger in one place, in one being.

It wasn't the girl. She was heartbroken, not angry. And she was on the outside, beyond where the shadows lay with their evil raging. She was in the dim light of the nether world.

A pretty girl with blonde hair that hung down around her face. She was pregnant. Oh, my indeed. Her whole belly sat like a medicine ball in her lap and she had her hands clasped around it, holding it, rocking back and forth and singing through her tears.

"Puff the Magic Dragon lived by the sea ..."

She was singing to the baby.

She became aware of him then and looked up.

This girl was a see-through. A translucent being with form and shape and color, but not substantial. You could see the dirty floor of the filthy shack through her. But between her and the floor was the insubstantial see-through reality of the bed where she sat.

"She's dead," the girl said to him. Her lips moved but the words didn't come at him through his ears but directly into his head. That part had been disconcerting, the first time that happened. He didn't realize until then how much voice mattered to speech. A man's voice, a woman's soft voice, the high giggle of a little child. When you only heard words in your head there was no voice. Some of the inflections of speech were there, but muted. No, not muted. They were flattened out, like a wrinkled shirt that had been poorly ironed.

"Who's dead?" he asked. He didn't even bother to speak the words out loud because she couldn't hear his voice any more than he could hear hers.

"My baby. It's a girl. I know it is. Robbie's mama says if you carry a baby high like I am, it's always a girl. Low babies is boys. It's a girl."

"What's her name?"

"Marilee. Marilee Winona Potter. Marilee just 'cause it's such a pretty name, and Winona for my Aunt Winona. Robbie said he wanted a boy and I told him I did, too, but I really didn't. I wanted a girl." She stopped, seemed to realize where she was or what was happening.

"She's not moving anymore. She's dead in there. I can feel it. A dead cold lump in my belly."

"It's cold where you are?"

She didn't answer that question either.

"When Selma first felt the queerness of it, me and Amelia went running into her room because she was moaning and carrying on. It was in there, taking her. And when we come in, it took us, too."

"What took you?"

"The Jabberwock. But wasn't no mirror, no mirage. It was just there. Dark and cold and I wanted to run away. It's hard to run when you're pregnant but I woulda … only I froze up and I couldn't, didn't go to the Dollar Store parking lot." She patted her belly. "Least she didn't have to stop breathing. I did. We did. Just stopped. Wasn't like we was choking or nothing, just we didn't need to breathe no more so we didn't. Little Marilee never did get to breathe, though. She died 'thout ever drawing a single breath of air."

She started to cry again and Moses moved closer to her. But not too close, though. He could feel a pull, a force, a power like one of those retractor beams in a science fiction movie that emanated from the darkness behind the ephemeral light where the girl was and he feared that if he stepped too close, it would take him, too, as it had taken Becky Sue.

The closer he got to her, the more he saw images around her, *from* her. Like she was too translucent to keep the world of her experiences inside, the barrier of who she was had become so thin her essence filtered out into the space around her.

Moses looked at the scenes.

Playing in the mud of a creek. Giggling. A freckle-faced boy picks up something brown and wiggling, a salamander, and tries to put it in her hair ...

The backseat of a car. The windows fogged. He touches her and she gasps, never knew anything felt like ...

A mirror, a mirage across a road. People standing, staring at it.

"Go ahead, cross it!" one teenage boy taunts another.

"I ain't ending up in the Middle of Nowhere puking my guts up."

A kitchen table. Three women, one older with stringy gray hair, one a pimply-faced teenager. "Where are they?" the teenager cries out. "Where's Aaron? Is he still up in Lexington? Why don't he come home?"

"Can't," the old woman says. "Makes sense, don't you think? If can't nobody leave, can't nobody come in neither."

A CROWD of people in a room with a stage, an auditorium. The rumble of voices, a man in a uniform speaks.

"I don't have to tell anybody in this room that something is happening here to all of us that has changed everything in our lives. We've all been dealing with it individually, in our own ways, but I believe it's time for us to figure out how we, all of us, as nowhere people need to respond as a group, doing together what none of us can do individually.

A woman named Charlie speaks. Someone says her mother used to make pottery.

"As we stay here, we vanish. It's happening right now. The Jabberwock consumes us, we cease to exist. You can't just sit back and make do with a life that ends at the county line. You better get up off your backside and start trying to figure out how to fight something that's going to eat you while you sit there."

THE NIGHT SKY, black velvet with stars. But the stars don't blink. They're all the same size, not some smaller and some bigger — uniform as lights on a Christmas tree. How can stars not blink?

A PRETTY TEENAGER, a black girl in a smock that has smiley faces on it. She's behind a counter. "It was rabid, almost tore poor E.J.'s leg off. And he can't get the shots. The Jabberwock ..."

MOSES REALIZED TOO late that he'd gotten too close to the pregnant girl on the floor. The magnetic pull of the darkness beyond her had grabbed hold and was pulling him relentlessly forward.

Oh, God, no.

What was there in the darkness, that *was* the darkness? It was the single most awful thing Moses had ever encountered, more full of hate and anger and vengeance, all blackness and boiling loathing. It was stronger than any evil Moses had ever encountered in the spirit world — the hate and anger and pain of many who had become one. It drew him relentlessly forward. It wanted him, it would have him. Not to take him cold and breathless to a translucent reality peopled with shadows. It would take him into the great maw of evil incarnate and it would devour his soul.

He whimpered. Wanted to plead, beg for his life, but he couldn't speak. And there was no pity there to seek. The being was … more than one, but all one. Behind the many were the one, but it was part of them, too, fueled them, drew strength from them. Sucked energy from the souls it devoured and grew. Bigger and bigger.

Moses Weiss had ventured too close. Too close.

When Duncan Norman leapt out into nothing, he yanked Malachi off his feet and in an instant of instinct, Malachi reached out and grabbed. It was all he had time to do. It wasn't enough, couldn't stop his fall, but he was able to snatch a moment's hold on the overhanging tree limb he had pushed out of his way when he stepped up beside Duncan. Only for a heartbeat before it was jerked out of his grasp, but it was long enough that Duncan's forward momentum carried him past Malachi and broke his grip on Malachi's hand so that he fell away and Malachi fell behind him.

No longer coupled to Duncan, without the minister's weight dragging at him, Malachi twisted sideways and he clutched at … everything, grabbed hold of nothing.

The spot on the mountainside where Duncan Norman had launched himself off the edge was not the smooth rock face of the overlook cliff. At the overlook, the drop was straight down, the vertical cliff face of solid rock was as smooth and flawless as if carved out of the mountain with a chisel in the hand of God. Returning World War II soldiers had commented it reminded them of the White Cliffs of Dover.

Duncan had dragged Malachi off a cliff, yes, but it was neither completely vertical nor smooth rock. It was a jagged, rugged mountainside, with jutting outcrops, cracks, crags and crevices. Scraggly trees grew near the top, even scragglier bushes grew out of cracks along the slope, and Kudzu vines covered much of it in a thick, green blanket.

Malachi banged into the protruding edges of jagged rock, crashed through vine-enshrouded bushes — grabbing frantically at anything and everything — catching only handfuls of leaves, scratching his fingers and skinning his knuckles as he bounced downward. It all went by in a flash. He hit a lump on the rock face that gouged pain into his side and he cried out, bounced off it, hit something else, slid rather than fell maybe fifteen feet, then off into nothing again.

Then he crashed down onto something on his back. Daggers of pain stabbed into his right hip and shoulder and his head slammed backward into the rough surface.

The world went black.

Chapter Twenty-Nine

MOSES WEISS LOOKS out eyes that are not his own.

They are alien, totally foreign and looking through them is similar to standing inside a tall building and looking out an open window on the world. A window so high it's above the level of the clouds and what lies below him is mist.

All that exists out beyond the window is down there where mist shrouds the universe.

The eyes that are not Moses's blink. And Moses is suddenly afraid, more afraid than he has ever been in his life. The fear is Moses's. It belongs to Moses and he owns it, clings to it as the only thing truly his and struggles against all that is not his in this bizarre reality.

He is furious, but the fury is not his. Except it is, because he can feel the heat of it coursing through his veins. The rage is an emotion so powerful, it blots out all else. Except the fear, the fear that belongs to Moses.

The rage is not some transient emotion, a reaction to some situation or circumstance. The rage is endemic to his being. Not Moses, the other.

Yes, Moses is within the other.

What little of his own mind he still possesses wonders if he has been absorbed, like whatever it was that happened to the people in Nowhere County, and if he has, will he be taken as they were taken to a somewhere that both is and isn't Nowhere County. A replica. A mirror image, the other side of a looking glass. A construct that occupies the same space but exists in time between seconds — so it is there and not there, two universes separated by less than a heartbeat. Time bent.

And that should jack up the fear that is his own, within the chest that is not his own. Being absorbed. Taken. Gone. He should be terrified of that, but it seems so far distant from his true terror. Like being in a doctor's office afraid of getting a shot ... when the whole building is on fire and all the exits are blocked and you are going to burn alive, screaming.

That fear, the one Moses owns, is fear of the other. The other through whose eyes he sees and whose emotions he feels.

And whose thoughts — tatters and scraps of them — he can hear.

Kill them, take them all. Chew them up.

Feed.

We will feed.

We will not be hungry.

Feed. He hears himself say the word out loud, hears the other speak the word into the real world.

And others of his kind say the word, too. Different voices — some high-pitched like a little child, some rumbling, the grumbling roar of an angry grizzly. Some in the stark-naked terror of a nightmare.

Moses hears the voices with ears that are not his own as the eyes through which he sees the world are the other's.

We will eat — I will eat whatever pleases me. I will feel the blood dripping down my chin, crush the bones with my teeth and suck out the marrow.

The others murmur agreement, but it is the one, the other, the Moses who is not Moses, the leader by virtue of his malignant loathing hatred and anger that propel them all forward.

He wants to give pain, he lives to give pain. He wants … payback.

Yes, payback.

He will visit on them more pain than all of them have felt — by a factor of ten. He will hear them scream. But he will cut off their screams because he could not scream. By that time, when the pain consumed him, he could no longer make a sound.

He will not grant them the release of giving voice to their misery. He will keep them silent. As he was silent.

As all the others were silent, leaving him alone.

The mist below the high window through which Moses looks begins to clear, and he can see that it is not a high window at all, that the mist was not clouds obscuring the earth far below, but a fine gathering of ground mist that flows out over the forests and meadows from streams. He sees the mist and strains to …

He wants … Wants!

Now, the morning mist is edging toward the crack through which he looks and his rage and hatred are replaced by desperate longing.

He is so thirsty. His mouth is dry, his lips cracked, and the mist is wet.

He leans his cheek against the cold surface that is one wall of the crack and tries to capture even a few drops of the mist, sticks his tongue out, struggles. But it is beyond his grasp. And he would cry, but he has no tears left.

And so he rages, hates, imagines taking, hurting, tasting blood. He bangs his fists on the wall beside the crack and his fists are raw from constant banging. He turns and looks back into the darkness behind him. He must feed. He rages at what he cannot have, but he is so hungry.

. . .

MOSES!

His cheek stung and his head snapped to the side. He opened his eyes into a reality not distorted by somebody else's eyes. He was sitting in the dirt. Dirt on wood. A dirty floor. The hundred-year-old house that wasn't.

"Look at me," Jolene said, "Look me in the eye!"

"Okay …" He looked Jolene in the eye.

"You're back. Sorry I had to slap you, but it was all I knew to do. What happened to you — do you know?"

He knew, but he couldn't speak of it. He had been sucked into … and had escaped. No, not escaped. He could never have escaped. There was no escape from that place. The Jabberwock had *let him go.* But it wasn't finished with him. Oh, no, it absolutely was not done with Moses Weiss.

He saw the others exchange a look, knew he ought to say something, but couldn't imagine what that might be.

"You fell down, sort of folded up on the floor — do you remember that?" Jolene asked. He shook his head. "You were sitting here with your eyes open, but Moses Weiss had definitely left the building."

"Left. Just so. *Gone.*" Moses shuddered because he understood the fundamental truth of what he was saying.

"Gone where?" Cotton asked.

"The thing, the Jabberwock … Too close, got too close. Just so. It sucked me in. I was part of it, in its mind. I saw." Moses actually shuddered again. "Inside it." He shook his head, muttered, more to himself than to the others. "And I am here to report that thing is *pissed!*"

A *whum, whum, whum* sound in his head, keeping time with his heartbeat. Familiar. Something rang his bell. Where …?

Sergeant McKenna calls out in a loud voice and Malachi struggles to hear him. The obstacle course, the rock wall. Lost his grip. Fell.

"I said, get up off your butt, Marine. There is no such thing as 'try.' You will not try to climb over that wall. You will *climb over that wall. You will hit it again and again and again until you're on the other side or one of us dies of old age."*

No, not that. His head was full of static, but his body understood that he could not move, that he was on some slanted surface and he must be still. Until his mind caught up with his muscle memory, he would remain frozen. He opened his eyes, the world swam dizzily in front of them so he closed them again.

A bar in Sarajevo, a drunk coming at him with a bottle of beer raised above his head.

An IED. It has blown the Armored Personnel Carrier off the road, must have thrown him and Hodgekiss out and now Hodgekiss is dragging him and he has to get his bearings …

No, not that. He was lying on his back, head below his feet, cold beneath, cold rock. He lifted his head and a wave of dizziness washed over him. The lights blinked out again.

When Malachi again opens his eyes, he is lying on his back in the transport truck, bouncing along the road toward the airport. His best friend, Charlie Blinkhorn, is leaning over him.

"I'm sorry, man, but I had to do it. You woulda shot all of 'em."

The man sitting next to him nods toward the front of the truck where the sergeant is sitting beside the driver. "But just one … Sarge is gonna say the guy attacked you and you had no choice but to shoot him."

Malachi's mind is spinning and he is so dizzy he can barely manage to keep his head up. He hears what the man is saying, but the words aren't yet connecting to reality in his mind.

The boy. Where is the boy?

He tries to rise.

"I got to get back to the boy," he says, as hands restrain him and push him back down onto the floor. Malachi fights with all his strength, which is no strength at all. His mind is caught in a loop. He has to get to the boy, find him, save him.

"Let me go. The boy—"

"Is dead, Malachi," Blinkhorn tells him. He pauses, sees Malachi still isn't tracking, and leans close to whisper into his ear. "The one with the sharp stick, he gave Sarge the little boy's head and told him to give it to you."

No, not … he wasn't in Rwanda.

This time he concentrated on not opening his eyes and not moving his head, on figuring out what was going on from other senses that wouldn't send him roiling back into the darkness.

His fingers could feel cold beneath. He rubbed gently. Rock. He was lying on a stone. Concrete? No, stone. He listened, could hear wind in trees, the distant rumble of artillery fire. No, not rumble. It was a buzz, not a rumble.

Cicadas. It was the buzz of cicadas in the bushes. He listened. Water running. A river, somewhere near a river. The intake of breath brought with it the smell of crushed greenery, his own fear sweat and ... honeysuckle.

He was in Kentucky. What had hap—?

Then he remembered. Understanding rocked him and his eyes popped open and he looked around, realized then that the slanted sensation was not a product of having his bell rung. He was lying on a slanted rock. If he moved, sneezed, maybe even if he lifted his head, he could start sliding right down it into ... nothing.

Chapter Thirty

S*TUART* W*ATCHED* the old man as he tried to speak, sputtered and muttered, his hands shaking so badly the coffee sloshed in his cup, the coffee he'd said he wanted, then told Jolene "no thank you" when she handed it to him, but nodded and took the cup anyway.

Stuart was trying very hard not to leap out of his own skin, not to jump up and down and cheer and yell and cry, and fall into a deep sleep for days.

All of the above at the same time and none of them.

In truth, he was as rattled and scattered as Moses Weiss. Rattled and scattered — sounded like a short-order cook's description of how he wanted his eggs. And "smothered," too. That meant put cheese on them.

They were alive. ALIVE.

The word banged around in Stuart's head and he realized he had a ridiculously silly grin on his face. Well, Jolene looked pretty chipper herself and so did Cotton. Moses had talked to the spirit of the pregnant girl, Becky Sue, had seen flashes of her memory, and she'd said the people of Nowhere County were alive. The three of them had been right. The people who'd vanished out of Nowhere County — the nobody-knew-how-many-thousands of them — had not all died in some cataclysmic event. They were just … gone.

Where? How? Yeah, he'd get to those questions. They all would.

They were, after all, the most important questions of their existence, but right now his mind was in what Coach Hawthorne had called "a continuous loop." You had to control your strength on the football field, somehow manage to go all-out, give it everything you had on every play and still have something left in the tank for the next play. And the next.

He had to rein in his excitement, focus … but right now, for just a few glorious minutes, he left his joy unchecked, let it run free.

Charlie and Merrie were alive!

Okay, he didn't know that for *sure* — that the two specific people who mattered most to him in all the world were among the people in Nowhere County who had not yet been gobbled up by the beast Moses had described in disjointed sentences that individually made no sense at all but taken as a whole fit together like an impressionist painting.

Moses paused to take a sip from the jiggling coffee cup in his hand and some of it dribbled down his chin. He didn't wipe it away.

"So you're saying the Jabberwock — and it is the Jabberwock, that was its name, right?" Cotton didn't wait for a reply. "It's a monster of pure evil, driven by absolute hatred and in a state of blind rage."

The old man blinked. "That about covers it."

"Okay, let's pull this wagon back up to the barn and load it all over again," Stuart said.

"Something your old granny used to say?" Jolene asked. Even Jolene had color in her face now, still favored her injured arm, but no longer looked like — what was it Cotton had said, "death on a cracker."

"My old granny wasn't a shucking-corn kind of grandmother. She worked fourteen hours a day in a sewing factory in Grixdale on the north side of Detroit. I just heard that phrase once in a movie and always wanted to use the line. Let's go over what we know, what we've learned."

He ticked the elements off on his fingers as he spoke.

"We know that wherever everybody is, they can't leave. They call the barrier—"

"It's on the county line, so that makes sense — the Jabberwock's like a wall on the border keeping everybody captive and on our side wiping away memories of Away-From-Heres when they leave," Jolene said.

"Away-From-Heres?" Moses asked, but Stuart blew by him.

"It looks like a mirage, and when you cross it, you … what?"

"Are transported into … nowhere," Moses said.

"No, to the Middle of Nowhere. It's a place, the Middle of Nowhere," Cotton said.

"And wherever they are, it's not … right. Not normal, the stars are off," Stuart said.

"They're trying, too, just like we are," Jolene put in. "Trying to figure this thing out, they all got together in a meeting to put their heads together."

"They recognize it, at least some of them do. They know they're vanishing and they're trying …" Cotton trailed off.

That statement drained all the energy out of the room, the power of their joy and excitement, knowing that the people they loved were alive somewhere. They were alive, might still be … no, they were, they still were alive … but they wouldn't be for long unless they could figure out how to beat this thing, this Jabberwock.

Jolene spoke. "What have we learned that helps us *figure it out?* What do we know now that we can use?"

"Well …" Stuart stretched his tired mind as best he could, willed it to put pieces of the puzzle together. "We know they had a meeting, a crowd of them, to talk, to pool what they knew." He paused. "What if … what if we could communicate with them, share what we know and what they know?"

"How?" Cotton asked.

"I'm just launching this out there, but … okay, there's somewhere that a lot of people got together."

"It had to be in the West Liberty Middle School auditorium, on Main Street in Persimmon Ridge," Cotton said.

"So people got together in a group there. Is there any way we could … talk to the group, or people in the group?"

"Like you did with Charlie in her kitchen?" Jolene asked. "And with the map and the black stickpins."

"Write them some kind of message?" Cotton asked. "Paint something on the wall? What are you suggesting?"

"I have no idea what I'm suggesting. Just thinking that a whole bunch of spirits in one spot … might be able … like Jolene said about the Jabberwock — could it really wipe the minds of hundreds of people? Like that. All we did was communicate with one person at a time — your father and my wife. What if we could try to communicate with a room full of people?"

"People were in the auditorium for a meeting — it's not like there are hundreds of people in it all the time," Jolene said.

"If they had one meeting, they will have others. If they plan to share information, they'd need to get together to do it. That auditorium ... how could we ...?"

"Like I said, write on the wall or the floor or ...?" Cotton said.

"I don't think anything we do here would ... it doesn't sound like what happens here is visible there," Jolene said. "Wherever they are, it's in a different ... place. We'd have to communicate somehow with something that's already in *both* places."

"Nothing left in any house or building in this whole county except what was on the walls — like maybe it was part of the building somehow," Cotton said. "Everything else inside the buildings is ... on their side, I guess. It's not on ours."

"Which is why the blackboard worked," Jolene said. "Both worlds."

"And the map," Cotton said.

"Soooo ..." Jolene wondered aloud.

"So we take the blackboard off the wall in Charlie's mother's kitchen and the map off the wall in your father's living room and we take them to that meeting room, put them on the wall there. And leave a message on them. Sometime ... eventually, I have to believe there'll be another meeting there, people in the room. and maybe ... maybe the messages will communicate."

"I think that's worth a shot," Cotton said, "but I'm going to try something else." He scratched his head. "The creature, the beast that Moses encountered ... pure evil, black, raging anger ..." Cotton paused. "So I'm thinking, 'How did that little girl get all chummy with the thing?' Lily Topple. She talked to it and it talked to her. We need to know more about that. I'm going back to have another talk with Rose, see if she can tell me why. And maybe tell me what the thing said to her mother."

"Jolene and I'll move the blackboard and the map while you—"

"We'll have to go back, you know that, don't you?" Jolene's voice was tight with fear. "Out there, to Gideon. All the roads lead there. That's where ... *it* is."

"Face it down? High Noon on Main Street – something like that?" Stuart said.

"Yeah, something like—"

"I need to go home now," the old man interrupted. His voice was soft, the commanding quality absent. He was in a daze, just sitting there at the table with them, and they'd pretty much forgotten about him.

"Moses, you aren't in any shape to go anywhere," Jolene said. "You can't hold a coffee cup; how can you drive a car?"

The man became unexpectedly hostile.

"Well, I suppose I shall just have to figure it out, won't I." He got to his feet, steady, like maybe his anger had firmed up his spine. "I was glad to come and give you a hand and all that, but I really must be getting back to Nashville now."

He stopped and the bluster left him.

"I want this ... all of this, *everything* out of my head!"

Stuart got it then. The old man knew that as soon as he crossed the county line, all his memories of what had happened here would be wiped away.

"You want to forget, don't you?" Stuart put his hand on the old man's arm.

No hostility now, he looked pleadingly into their faces.

"Yes, oh my yes. I want it gone. I want to go home and not remember any of this happened to me."

"I get that, but still ..." Jolene didn't like it, but it wasn't her decision to make.

They talked about it, decided that it would be best if Jolene wrote a note for Moses to carry with him explaining to him that they'd spoken and some weird things had happened that he wouldn't remember, but that he should go on home and she'd give him a call and explain the whole thing in a few days.

Once he'd made up his mind, the decision apparently caught his pants on fire because Moses Weiss was suddenly in a great hurry. Jolene quickly scrawled the note and the three walked him out to his car. They didn't have any scotch tape, so they used the surgical tape Cotton had gotten for Jolene's bandages, and taped the note to the center post of the steering wheel where he couldn't miss it.

"Moses, are you sure you're up to—?"

"Certainly. Just so. Absolutely sure. I must go, now. So sorry to leave you here with all this, but I can't ... I can't be here any longer."

The old man shook hands all around, got into his car and drove away a little too fast down Chimney Rock Pike toward Elkhorn Road. Cotton'd given him directions. Stuart hoped he remembered them.

Jolene said softly, "I don't like this."

"Neither do I," said Cotton.

"Three of a kind," Stuart confirmed, then turned to go back into the house for his car keys. "But we have work to do."

Cotton followed. Jolene stood where she was, watched until Moses Weiss's car disappeared around a curve.

~

THE WORLD HAD STOPPED SPINNING, and the pain points Malachi felt brought reality into crisp focus. There was likely a goose egg the size of a medicine ball on the back of his head, where he had slammed down on the rock. There was a stabbing agony in his shoulder. He might have landed on it. He recognized the agony. He had dislocated his shoulder before and this was perilously close to that.

Maybe bruised ribs, hopefully not broken.

He could see up and to both sides without moving his head. Could see the top of the ridge above him. He'd obviously hung up on a rock outcrop.

Duncan Norman? He could be nearby, in a bush or hung around a tree or a rock. But it was much more likely he was down there, two hundred feet below the top of the ridge in the Rolling Fork River that Malachi could hear bubbling far below him. The man had leapt outward, had sprung off the cliff like those cliff divers in Acapulco. Malachi had banged down the face of the cliff, bouncing off it on his way down, but Duncan probably didn't hit anything in his descent. Until he hit the rocks in the river.

Slowly, Malachi moved his head to look at his swollen left shoulder and realized it hadn't totally dislocated, had just hyperextended, pulled the ball painfully away from the socket, but not totally out of it.

He also realized that his head was below the level of his feet, which had given him a distorted sense of the slope of the rock. He eased to the right slowly, taking the pressure off his left arm twisted beneath him, and with a groan of pain felt the arm shift back into the socket. Now, he needed to scoot slowly on his back, reorient himself, get his head above the rest of his body, and hope that when he did, the heartbeat *whum, whum, whum* in the lump on his skull would ease off.

Take it slow. Just scoot. It probably took him ten

minutes but he was finally lying level, horizontally on the slanted rock with the rock face on his right. Then he continued to scoot until his upper body was next to the rock face and his lower body was below him. The incline was too steep to even attempt to get to his hands and knees, but he had spotted a crack, a large fissure in the rock that ran up the cliff face. He inched that way across the rough surface of the rock and the tangle of vines that covered it. The vines were not strong enough to hold his weight, but grabbing a handful at least helped him balance, gave him a — probably false — sense of stability.

The crack in the cliff face ran alongside the slanted outcrop where he lay. When he reached the edge of the outcrop, he felt around with his right hand until he found the edge of the crack — and grabbed hold. He could hold onto the rock, wasn't going to slide downward as long as he held on.

He lay there, luxuriating in the sense of stability — not false, this time — that his hand hold granted him. Then he scooted a few more inches, shoved his hand down into the crack and made a fist. His fist held him firm.

He unclenched the fist and walked his fingers spider fashion up the inside of the crack, it was jagged, provided hand holds, and he was able to pull himself up, slowly, inching his way, until he was in a sitting positing on the slanted rock, his feet out in front of him, his right arm jammed into the crack with his fingers holding onto a shelf of rock.

He slowly turned this head then and for the first time looked over his left shoulder, let his eye travel down the slanted rock surface. It wasn't nearly as big a slab of rock as he'd thought and he was grateful he hadn't realized that. He could see off the edge of it, but it blocked the view directly below it. Maybe that's where Duncan had landed because he was nowhere Malachi could see.

Panting, sweating, Malachi quickly realized that trying to climb down was not an option. If he dared try to move down the rock face, he would slide right off the end of it and drop … onto whatever was below it.

Nope. The only escape was *up*.

Chapter Thirty-One

Sam heard the commotion out in the hallway, shouting voices, angry and frightened. The door to Rusty's room burst open and Raylynn got out only a couple of words, "Viola Tackett's here and her daughter—"

Then Neb Tackett shoved her aside.

"It's Essie, she's hurt, bleeding real bad!" He was wearing only a pair of jeans, no shirt. And a shirtless fat man was never an appealing sight even without the smears of blood that covered Neb's chest. "You got to see to her!"

A flush of anger rushed over Sam at the demanding tone. She wouldn't be commanded to leave Rusty by Neb Tackett or anybody else.

"Take her into Exam B. Raylynn will show you where to—"

Viola Tackett appeared in the doorway beside her son. Must be Sam's Viola Tackett day — this was the woman's third appearance. But she looked very different now. The swagger and self-assurance were gone. Her face was pale, drawn, and scared. And the front of her shirt was soaked in blood.

"Essie's been shot," she announced without preamble. Viola Tackett didn't mince words. "She needs help. Com'on — *now!*"

Sam snapped.

"I don't take *orders* from you, Viola Tackett! Maybe the rest of the world does, but I *don't*. My son needs me, too, and—"

The change in Viola's demeanor was stunning. She looked surprised at the outburst. Then shot her eyes to the bed and back to Sam.

"I didn't mean no harm. I'll sit with the boy if needs be, but my Essie's bleeding bad. Gut shot."

I'll sit with the boy if needs be?

Surely, Sam had heard her wrong.

But the words "bleeding" and "gut shot" got Sam moving. In truth, she had refused to leave Rusty's side not because he needed her but because she needed to be there. She couldn't do a thing for him but look at him, hold his hand, *will* him to open his eyes.

"Is Judd Perkins out there?" It was about time for the E.J. shift change and Sam thought she'd heard Judd's voice in the hallway.

Viola turned and looked down the hall, called out, "Yo, Judd. Come here. Sam needs you." Sam came out of Rusty's room, brushed past Viola and Neb and said to Judd, who was hurrying her way, "Would you sit with Rusty? Come get me if ... just sit there." She didn't wait for a reply, just said to Raylynn, who was standing in the suddenly crowded hallway, "Is Malachi back yet?"

"No, he—"

"Then, would you take E.J.?" She didn't wait for an answer to that question either, just turned to Viola. "Where's Essie?"

"She's out front in the bed of the truck."

Sam took off for the waiting room and the chubby woman kept up with her long stride step for step.

"What happened? How did—?"

"She was sitting on the porch and somebody come by and shot her."

Shot? *Shot!* What was *wrong* with people? All the violence — shootings, bashed-in skulls — *why* …?

Then Viola answered the question Sam hadn't asked. "I don't know who t'was done it, but I *will* find out!"

Bursting out into the squinty-bright sunlight, Sam found a fancy black pickup truck she was sure the Tacketts had stolen from somebody. The tailgate was down and Essie Tackett was lying on her back in the bed of the truck. Obie was on his knees beside her, holding her hand.

Sam climbed up into the truck and knelt beside the girl. She was pale, her breath shallow. Sam took her wrist to feel for a pulse, didn't count it, just wanted to see if it was strong. It wasn't. It was faint, rapid and thready. She didn't touch the wad of cloth — a tee-shirt, maybe, which would explain why Ned was bare-chested. The cloth, held to the girl's midsection by a buckled belt, was soaked in blood.

Sam scooted out of the truck to the pavement.

"Bring her inside," she told Essie's brothers. Then she ran into the building to make sure there were enough of the supplies she needed in the exam room — the one with a metal tray table designed so it'd be easy to clean off dog pee instead of a padded table covered in white paper.

As one part of her mind ticked off the specifics of bandages and other things she'd need, another part was speaking harsh truth. Even under the best of circumstances — with a trauma center, surgery and surgeons — a shot to the belly was about as bad as it got. Depending on the caliber of the bullet — well, actually, that hardly mattered.

Whatever the bullet, it had torn through the girl's intestines — coils of them, so there would be multiple entrance and exit wounds, all of them releasing fecal material into the body cavity. It was almost impossible, even for a surgeon, to suture multiple sites of damaged tissue and not miss one, and then clean the area well enough to prevent infection. E. coli infection, but there'd be others. Sepsis.

Sam had seen it once — a little girl had come into the emergency room of the University of Kentucky Medical Center. She had been camping with her family, tripped, fell and impaled herself on a tent stake, which punctured her abdomen almost all the way through to her back. She was in surgery for nine hours. They'd pumped enough antibiotics into her to … but it didn't matter. Infection set in. She died, and it was a grizzly death.

Essie needed surgery to … everything. To stop the internal bleeding. To disinfect the area. Sam couldn't help her. A sense of helplessness washed over her so profound that her step actually faltered and she stumbled before regaining her balance.

She couldn't help E.J. No rabies vaccine.

She couldn't help Douglas Taylor. No snakebite antivenom.

She couldn't help Rusty. No … whatever he needed.

And she couldn't help Essie Tackett. The girl would die. There was nothing Sam could do to prevent it. If she somehow managed to survive the gunshot wound, she would die of the resulting infection.

Stopping at the supply closet, she began grabbing extra bandages and tape. Suddenly, Viola Tackett was beside her.

"She gone die, ain't she."

It was more a statement than a question. Viola's voice was almost emotionless. Sam charitably chose to believe she was holding onto her feelings, not that she simply didn't have any.

She turned to face the old woman, marveled at how she had produced a son who resembled her, and yet the features were muted to make his face as strikingly handsome as hers was homely.

"You don't got to say nothing. I can see it in yore eyes. You can't fix her, can you?"

"No. I'm sorry. I can't."

"How long's she got?"

Sam knew she had to provide some kind of answer. The girl's mother was entitled to that, though the stark truth was that Essie might be dead already, or she might live a couple of days.

"My guess — and it's just a guess, Viola, there's absolutely no way to know — but I'm thinking … hours. Two or three, maybe. I can't stop the internal bleeding, so it depends on how much damage the bullet did."

"She gone bleed to death — that the way of it?"

"Yes."

"Is she in pain? Essie ain't good at telling you when—"

"I'm sure she is in pain. But we have" — she paused only briefly but the pause wasn't lost on Viola — "Oxycontin, and we can make her comfortable. It'll make her sleepy, too, of course, so she probably won't be able to talk—"

"She can't talk even when she ain't on drugs. That big fat ole tongue in her mouth, it garbles everything she says."

"But if *you* talk to *her,* she'll hear you. You can hold her hand and talk to her while I clean the wound."

"What you cleaning the wound for if she's gone die anyway?"

"Because that's what I *do!*" Sam snapped. She took a breath. "It's not much, but it's all—"

"I get it. You clean her up and bandage her. I'll be in there directly."

Viola turned on her heel and went to the door of the exam room where Essie'd been taken, crowded by the large bodies of her three sons, and said something. Zach came to the door and she walked down the hallway with him, talking rapidly, gesturing with her hands. Then Viola turned around and went back into Essie's exam room and Zach went down the hallway toward E.J.'s office. That was odd, but Sam let it go. She had bigger fish to fry.

As soon as Sam stepped into the exam room she evicted Obie and Neb. They were so large they made the room seem airless. Besides, she did *not* need the sight of Neb's bare belly right now and both of them smelled bad. Particularly Neb, who smelled like … urine. Viola was on the far side of the exam table, holding Essie's hand.

"I need my Malachi to be here. You know where he's at?"

"It's like I told you before. He took Reverend Norman out to Scott's Ridge to get his car."

"Shoot, it don't take all morning to get to Scott's Ridge and back. He musta gone some place after. Where might that be?"

Sam shrugged. But she'd been thinking the same thing. What was taking Malachi so long?

Chapter Thirty-Two

Malachi Tackett owed his life to a crack in a rock.

A big crack in a big rock.

The rocky face of the cliff that Duncan Norman had leapt off, dragging Malachi along with him, was cracked and fissured. One crack in the rock ran in a jagged line up the rock face from below the point where Malachi had slammed down onto a narrow rock outcrop to within twenty or thirty feet of the top of the cliff. It varied in width from a couple of inches to a couple of feet.

Malachi was *not* a sport rock climber. He had *endured* the rock-climbing aspect of Marine training that some recruits turned into an activity they enjoyed for years afterward. He'd gone along with friends a couple of times. Not his gig. And the *sport* of rock climbing differed in significant ways from "desperation" rock climbing, which was what Malachi was practicing as he struggled to inch his way up to the top of the cliff face on Ironwood Mountain.

In sport rock climbing, you got points for form. You didn't drag your upper body over the edge of some mountain peak on your belly, hauling the rest of your exhausted self over the final hump by crawling forward in panting relief. Oh no, you kept your back straight, lifted with your arms, stepped gracefully up onto the summit.

In sport rock climbing, you got to select the difficulty level, so you could choose to climb only what you were capable of climbing.

In sport rock climbing, you were strapped into a harness and dangling from a rope. You affixed yourself to the cliff face every ten or fifteen feet with various pieces of rock-climbing equipment. As you climbed, the rope ensured that you were never in danger of falling any farther than the last piece of protection.

Malachi was in danger of falling every second now, every breath could topple him and the difficulty level of the climb was far above his pay grade.

Once he could open his eyes without getting dizzy, he scooted on his back slowly, pivoting so that his head was finally above his feet on the slanted rock. Then he inched himself into a sitting position with his back against the cliff face.

Don't look down. Never look down.

But down was the only place there was to look. Correction. Out over the vast expanse of Dragonroot Hollow was the only place to look, but the ground there was *down* — waaaaay below his current elevation. Without leaning out over the edge of the rock outcrop — which he had no intention of doing — he couldn't see what was directly below him, the base of the cliff and the riverbank. He could only assume that Duncan Norman was ... that Duncan's *body* was lying somewhere down there.

The rock crack ran right alongside where he sat, snaking up the cliff face. He scooted upward, with his back against the cliff, until he was standing. Then he could reach his left hand into the crack. The edges were only a couple of inches wide at that point, but it widened as he stuck his hand farther into it. He shoved his hand as deep into the crack as he could and made a fist — which wouldn't fit back through the opening of the crack's edges. That secured him in place and he turned his body veeeeery carefully around until he was facing the cliff. With ever-so-gentle movements, he toed off his shoes and socks. They were running shoes with thick rubber soles. He had to be able to feel for toe holds with his feet the same way he'd feel for hand holds with his fingers. Besides, the shoes were so wide he couldn't even have jammed them into the crack. He placed his bare feet into the crack, jamming them in sideways, one at a time, and then balanced on them, his body held to the rock face by his fist in the crack. The rocks had already sandpapered the skin off the top of his hand and fore-arm, then off both feet. His toes pinched painfully in the narrow space.

He started up.

Reaching as high as he could in the crack, he felt around, his fingers searching for any irregularity he could grasp. When he found a hand hold, he carefully moved his feet, one after the other, out of the crack and jammed them into a higher spot, *pulling* himself upward with the hand hold and *pushing* himself up with his legs, balanced on his jammed-into-the-crack feet.

Time came completely unhooked from reality. He had been there an hour. Or five hours. Or thirty minutes. Or two days. This wasn't about wonky Jabberwock time, it was about the telescoping of normal time under dangerous conditions. He'd been there before. The adrenaline that fear dumped into his body gave him the strength and endurance he needed, but as it wore off, his muscles ached. His scraped feet bled, joined by raw, bleeding hands and fingers, the right hip and shoulder he'd landed on hurt and the knot on the back off his head throbbed.

Sweat ran into his eyes and he had no hand to wipe it away.

Life, existence, his whole world shrank to the rock right in front of his nose, his fingers frantically searching around for something to grasp, something to use to pull himself upward.

At one point, his foot, slick with blood, slipped as he was trying to reposition it in the crack and for a desperate few seconds, he was held to the mountainside by nothing more than his fingers' grip on a three-inch ledge of rock.

At another point, he searched as high as he could reach with his hands and found nothing but smooth rock. No hand hold, not the slightest dent in the surface. His leg muscles were quivering with fatigue, but he took the only chance he had. He thrust himself violently upward with his feet to extend his reach, fingers scrabbling, searching for … there was a crack in the smooth rock in the back of the crack he was climbing. It wasn't even two inches wide, but he jammed the four fingers of his right hand into it, and crimped his fingers, holding himself in place with the pressure of his knuckles against the rock.

Then the crack ended. Above it was smooth rock, and about four feet beyond that was a bush, old and gnarled, growing out of a crevice to the right. Either Malachi trusted that the bush would hold him … and if it didn't …

He moved his feet up the crack until he was crouched at the top of it, then in a single explosive move, he straightened up and shoved off with his feet, his hands out, grasping for the bush.

For a breathless moment he was off balance, his weight shifting back away from the rock. Away and downward.

Then he snatched hold of the bush, grabbed a handful of limbs, felt it give, then hold firm.

He grabbed the bush with both hands then and hauled himself slowly up the smooth rock face beneath it, his knees skinning along the rock.

He hugged the bush to his chest as soon as he could. It was the farthest down of the bushes that grew just below the top of the cliff, and he dragged himself from that bush to the next one above it, clawed and scrabbled and crawled up through the bushes until he was able to shove himself belly first onto the rocky top of the cliff.

He got no points for form, just crawled on his belly until he could get first one knee and then the other over the edge, then shoved himself forward until his whole body was lying on the rocks at the top.

He lay there, panting, sweating, his heart pounding out of his chest. When he caught his breath, he didn't trust himself to stand, so he crawled away from the cliff's edge into the trees, then sat, leaning his back against a gnarled oak, looking out over the vista.

He used the tree to pull himself to his feet and staggered away from the cliff. He probably ought to have gone to the edge and looked over, tried to see if he could see Duncan. Call out to him. Or at least locate Duncan's body. But he could not force himself to go anywhere near the cliff's edge, just lurched from one tree to the next to the parking lot and staggered across it to Charlie's car. His legs were weak and wobbly from exertion and when he pulled open the driver's side door, he plopped into the seat, then slowly turned and lifted both feet onto the floorboard.

He leaned his head on the steering wheel. And maybe he sobbed.

Chapter Thirty-Three

Rose had known who it'd be soon's they told her about the visitor. Knew it'd be that Cotton Jackson again, of course it was, had to be. Stink Bug had told her she didn't have to see him today, that they could make him come back tomorrow. He was supposed to give a whole twenty-four-hour notice when he called, and he hadn't done it. She'd told Stink Bug to go suck an egg.

He'd said last time he was here that everybody in Nowhere County had vanished in a puff of smoke, disappeared. Just like them folks, her mother's kin, done in Gideon a century ago. She'd been thinking about that Jackson fella ever since he left. Knew he wasn't done asking her things, that'd he'd be back wanting to know more stuff. She hadn't decided yet if she was gonna tell him or no.

Stink Bug knocked softly on her door and then opened it even those Rose didn't say nothing about her coming in.

"Mr. Jackson is at the reception desk, asking if he can speak to you. Are you sure—?"

"What, you think I changed my mind since I told you not half an hour ago that it was fine by me to have a visitor? You'd save yourself a whole lot of trouble if you'd just listen the first time."

The woman turned and walked away a huff.

The man knocked on the doorjamb of her open door, stood there polite until she said he could come in. He looked awful, like he hadn't slept a wink since the last time she talked to him. He looked worn thin, not his skinny body, but his whole self worn thin, like he was rubbed down to almost nothing at all.

He just didn't understand, didn't realize that wouldn't matter what she told him or didn't tell him, what he done or didn't do, the Jabberwock was gonna do whatever it wanted to do. She tried to tell him that, but he was bound and determined to find out about her mama and the Jabberwock.

She hadn't never shared that part, hadn't never told a living soul, had kept those secrets tucked away in her heart her whole life, ever since her mother told her about them when Rose was a little girl.

And told her. And told her.

Everything Mama said about that time, she repeated again and again. Rose supposed she didn't have nothing else but that to talk about, or might be she done it because she wanted Rose to remember, told her so many times so she wouldn't forget.

And she didn't forget. Them memories filled her mind just like they was her very own.

LILY TOPPLE CRAWLS along the ground, bent over so her face is only inches above the forest floor. Slow as she can go, she plows a path about two feet wide through the blanket of leaves, lifts each leaf, one at a time until she gets down to bare dirt. She picks up every object as she comes to it — every rock, stick, twig, stem, bug, beetle, worm, cater-

pillar, pebble, acorn or pinecone — and lays it aside in the bare-dirt trench on her right, the ground she's already cleared. She's careful that the path she is now plowing along the forest floor butts up perfectly against the one she cleared in her last pass, not so much as an inch of it unexamined.

When she finds one, or anything she thinks might be one, she puts it in the basket she drags on the ground behind her — the one Mama'd been making. Mama and some other ladies would sit on rocks by the waterfall in the cool of the evening, talking about everything and nothing, listening to the rush of water, weaving the strips of oak bark together. Lily's mother had already made a big basket of willow limbs — big enough for Lily to climb into and sit down — and that's where she kept the strips of oak bark. Both the baskets, the big one and the unfinished one — were still sitting where Mama'd left them beside that rock when Lily came back into town after she spent the night in the woods.

Lily washes off everything she finds and then examines it in bright sunlight. And if she isn't sure, she puts it in the duffel bag with the others just in case.

She is careful, oh, so very careful, because she can't miss a single one. Not one. And the little finger on a kid, a two-year-old maybe, isn't very big at all.

Her back hurts. She is hot and tired, the sun beats down on her through breaks in the trees and she considers giving up. Like she considered it yesterday and the day before. She's done listened to all the arguments in her head a dozen times.

Wasn't no reason to do such a thing, pick up all them bones — what for?

Wasn't no way she could find them all, even if she decided to try. Bones was little things, some of them, and she wasn't rightly sure what bones looked like, not all of them anyway. Everybody could pick out a skull, of course, but some bones like a little toe. What did that look like? And she couldn't gather them up if'n she didn't even know what she was looking for.

And what then? When she found them all, what then? What's she s'posta do with them? What's the point in finding the bones if she ain't got nothing to do with them once she done it?

There are other arguments besides those, lots more, but she has gotten so accustomed to ignoring them that the little ones finally give up trying to convince her. The bigger arguments still try now and then, though, particularly like now, when she is hot and tired, and knows there are many many more hours of daylight and she must use every minute. As she has used up all the minutes of every day since she made the decision. How long has it been? Days. Some days. Not weeks, she doesn't think. But could be. It doesn't matter. If it takes her a week or a month or a year ... doesn't matter. She has purposed in her heart to do the thing, and the difficulty or the time it takes don't matter. She'll do it 'cause she said she would. Pa had raised her that way. You done what you purposed in your heart to do and the least she could do, now that Pa and the others was gone, was be the kind of person he'd intended her to be when he was teaching her all them lessons.

She knows this is what Pa'd want her to do. That's why, the only reason why that makes any sense. Her Pa had tried to talk them others out of scattering the bones of the Jitter Dancers, said it wasn't right, that they ought not do such a thing. Her Pa was maybe the only miner in the whole camp who'd flat out refused to participate.

He'd said he wouldn't do a wrong thing like that. So she knows in her heart he approves of her trying to set it right.

And there is the other reason.

Maybe the bones ... maybe scattering the bones is why ...

There had to be a why, didn't there? She had sat huddled in a corner of her empty house for days, not doing nothing but trying to figure out what had happened to all them people. And why it had happened.

The mine foreman didn't know. Mr. Tackett had come looking, of course, when didn't none of the miners show up for work, got all up in arms about it. She was sure he'd do something. But he only come that one time and never returned.

She was just a little girl, not even a woman yet, so what did she know? But them bones … was it about them bones? The company man made them get rid of the bones and the next morning the whole town was … gone. Was that why?

And the haints — Lily knows they's real because she's heard their wail … Is it possible that maybe the haints is all that's left of the people them bones used to be? Haints was in cemeteries, the ghosts of dead people. So did these bones have ghosts, too, but out there in the woods since they'd been buried in a cave 'stead of a cemetery? Was it their ghosts that wailed in misery at night, raising the hair on the back of her neck with their mournful cries?

Lily never does settle the whole thing in her mind. She just does what seems right to do.

Her Pa thought them bones ought to be respected. Well, she could do that. She could do that much for her Pa. And if them bones was somehow the reason the vanishing happened … then maybe if she gathered them all up. Maybe …

And so every day she ignores the voices in her head that try to convince her that her effort is wasted. That ain't no use to be doin' what she's doing. Every day, all day, she combs the forest floor. She made herself a plan 'fore she ever started, gathered up rocks and used them to mark out lines through the trees so she wouldn't miss nothing. Wasn't a big stand of woods, but it was thick and there was lots of brush. She works from the time the sun clears the top of Hazzard Bluff to the east until it's too dark to see. Stops only to pee and eat — a small portion of meat from the smoke house that didn't vanish, fruit, berries and mushrooms — Pa taught her how to tell the good ones from the ones that'd make you sick.

Springtime turns into summer and the leaves is starting to turn them pretty colors and fall off the trees before she has searched all the woods where the miners went. Every inch.

She is certain she has every bone that Rufus Giddings'd spotted in that burial cave, the bones Mr. Tackett dumped out of the duffle bags on the ground in front of Mr. Milliken.

She finishes the last bit at sunset and goes to bed, curled up in a ball on the floor where her bed had been, in the empty house where she'd lived with her family all around her, with the town all around her, until …

The next morning, she walks around the stand of woods, checkin' to make sure there is no area she has neglected to search.

Nope. She has them all.

She sits down, gathering herself for what comes next, on the bottom step of the house where the Finneys lived. It's so close to the Carthage Oak it is in the shade all day long. It will be a long, hard haul, carrying the duffle bags she has filled with bones up the mountainside. She had best get to it.

ROSE'S MAMA Lily had told her where she took the pile of bones and what happened after she done it. And what she did then — because the Jabberwock told her to. Rose hadn't never told anybody about any of that.

Chapter Thirty-Four

MOSES GOT LOST five minutes after he left Cotton Jackson's house.

And so he drove down one winding mountain road after another. For half an hour or five hours or ten minutes — he didn't know. There were no road signs, or they were so full of bullet holes they were unreadable. Why would you use a road sign for target practice? And even if there had been signs, Jolene had laid out for him a different route back to Nashville than the way he'd come. She'd said it was the best way to go and he hadn't argued with her because he didn't want to spend the time arguing. He wanted to leave. Had to leave. Had to get out of there, away from that house, those people.

The imperative to flee now, now, *now* was thrumming so loud in his head he had trouble concentrating on what she'd said. On his way to Nower County, he had taken Interstate 65 North to near Bowling Green, then some parkway east, he couldn't remember the name of it — Nunn something. He'd gotten confused on it because it'd just ended in some place called Somerset and he'd had to find another road to another place called London and from there took another parkway, the Rogers parkway, he thought, east into the Kentucky mountains.

Jolene had said it would be less confusing if he merely went back to London — he'd told her he was sure he could find that, but he had been bluffing, he wasn't sure at all — and then take Interstate 75 from London due south to Knoxville. Straight line, can't get lost. And then Interstate 40 due west from Knoxville to Nashville. He'd find his way home once he got to Tennessee. Or maybe he wouldn't. He didn't care a fig about that. All he wanted was *out of Nower County.* All he wanted was to cross the county line … and forget it all! He could wander aimlessly around after that, he didn't care, just so long as he couldn't remember …

Feeeeeed, he says again.

It *says again.*

The rage washes over him in a tide that carries him away through the night, through a darkness of mind where no light ever shines. Rage and hatred.

The hatred is a pure black thing that is so tangled up with the rage that they are almost the same thing.

The Moses who is not Moses hates the people, loathes them, despises them. Wants to rip them apart with his bare hands and feed on them.

Feed.

We will not be hungry, he says in unison with the other voices. Never be hungry again.

MOSES REALIZED that he had crossed the center line and was driving on the wrong side of the road. The images had filled his head, momentarily blinding him. No traffic, though, no cars on the road. Empty. No one there, all gone, vanished. He pulled back to the right side and concentrated as hard as he could on keeping the car where it should be. On the winding mountain roads a single mistake, a jerk of the wheel, could send him through a guardrail and off into nothing.

Maybe that's what he should do. Not much effort. A little jerk, close his eyes. It would be over quick. And then it would truly be all over. All the spirits, all the dead people and their pain. All over.

Perhaps he should end it. Definitely something he ought to give serious consideration, yes, just so. But not until he got the monster out of his head, not until he was just Moses Weiss, *only* Moses Weiss, the man who talked to dead people … and not the being inside the pure evil thing, looking out its eyes, wanting death, blood, to feed.

So he drove.

And drove.

Significant time passed, though he wasn't able to measure it, didn't have a watch. The shadows of the mountains all around him lengthened, and the pools of darkness under the trees grew blacker. Rabbit Run Road. A sign, an actual readable sign said he was on Rabbit Run Road. Not good. Oh, dear, no, not good at all. He had already been on Rabbit Run Road! Of course he had. He knew he had because the road actually had a sign and none of the other roads had signs. He was going in circles. That understanding yanked the knot in his belly tighter. He was a mouse in a maze, going around and around, desperate to find a way out. But all the roads looked the same. How did the people who lived here find their way when the roads were all the same and there were no signs?

But there were no people in Nowhere County, lost or otherwise. They'd all vanished.

He kept driving, turned off Rabbit Run Road as soon as he could onto some other road that had no name. He turned right off that road onto one that did have a sign dangling sideways on a pole.

Ravel Witch Hwy.

The bullets had blasted some of the letters off the sign. Maybe a C before "ravel." Cravel? Or a G. Gravel. Yes, probably Gravel. Gravel Witch Highway. Only there was definitely a missing letter in front of witch. Totally obliterated, gone. A guess — Kwitch? Pwitch? Switch. S, yes. Gravel Switch made sense. Except it didn't because what was a Gravel Switch?

His mind was ping-ponging and he couldn't seem to grab hold of it, force it to be still, to think, to concentrate. He was going in circles and he'd never get out of here if he kept doing that and he had to get away. Away. *Away.* Had to cross the county line and have the memories wiped away.

He began to cry.

At some point, he switched on his headlights. It was dangerous to drive as fast as he was driving on these mountain roads at night! But he met no cars, passed no cars.

All the people here had vanished, you see. Right, vanished. The Jabberwock. *No!* If he thought about that he would go insane.

But maybe he already had gone insane.

Suddenly, his headlights illuminated a sign that he thought said, "Crawford County, one mile." Hard to tell with all the bullet holes. He hadn't been on this road before, though — he didn't think. Maybe ... maybe escape wasn't far. Sweet joy rose up in his chest. He remembered noticing the Welcome to Nower County sign when he drove through, saw how someone had used red paint to add letters, an H and an E, making Nower County NowHerE County and he'd smiled at that.

He smiled now, too, as he saw the back of a sign come into view on the other side of the road that might very well say "Welcome to Nower County" on the front. Not far, only a little way and then it would be gone, all over. Stuart and Cotton had promised that he would remember absolutely nothing about what had happened here as soon as he crossed the county line. Mere seconds now and the knot of terror in his belly would untie itself, though he supposed that when it did he'd wonder, "What was I so anxious about?" That broadened his smile and he reached down and patted the piece of paper affixed with surgical tape to the center of the steering wheel.

Closer. Closer.

As his car flew past the sign, Moses fell into a black nothingness that sparkled like black glitter. He could see in the blackness as if it were light. Black light. He heard a sound … no, he didn't hear it. Hearing happened in your ears, not in your toes and your knees and your elbows — your whole body. A sound like static invaded every cell, a mighty, fuzzy, buzzing sound filled up his whole being, so loud-but-not-loud it loosened his teeth.

The dark and the sound ate up his world and Moses Weiss and his car vanished off the road as if it had never been there at all.

Chapter Thirty-Five

WHAT COULD Cotton say to entice Rose Topple to open up and tell him the rest of her mother's secrets?

He had spent the drive from his home on Chimney Rock Pike through Persimmon Ridge on Wiley Road, then up Route 15 to Carlisle in Beaufort County and the Aspen Grove Nursing Home trying to figure that out. He found himself knocking on the door jamb of her open door, looking at the shriveled old woman in the bed, still clueless. So much was riding on the information locked in the old woman's head and if he couldn't unlock it …

"Come on in and sit yourself down and next time you come you best give them the twenty-four-hours notice they want or they ain't gonna let you in the door. They love to turn folks away. It's a power thing; they shove you around to show you that they in charge and you ain't."

Cotton crossed the room and sat in the chair she'd indicated.

"I ain't gone ask what I can do for you. I didn't fall off a hay truck yesterday, you know. You come here to talk about Mama."

"I've spent the past half hour trying to think what I could say to talk you into telling me the rest of what you know."

"What'd you come up with."

"Nothing. Either you'll tell me or you won't. All I can do is ask."

"So ask."

"Why did the Jabberwock leave your mother alone? It took the whole town, but then let one little girl live there … for years. You said it was because she 'done right by it.' You said the Jabberwock talked to your mother. I want to know … I *need* to know what it said to her."

"*Need* to know?"

Cotton lost it then.

"I'm trying to save the lives of thousands of people, so yes, I *need* to know!" He knew he'd stepped in it then. Her whole face closed up, like she'd slammed doors and locked windows. He tried to backtrack. "I'm sorry, I didn't mean to …" He took a breath, looked at her expressionless face. Then he just let it out. "Look, I'm too tired and too scared to be polite! A whole county full of people has vanished just like Gideon did a hundred years ago. If I can't figure out something to do, some way to … I don't know, talk to the Jabberwock or deal with it or … *I don't know what!*" He drew in a ragged breath and tried to speak more softly. "All I *do* know is that unless I do something, Stuart's wife and little girl, Charlie and Merrie — she's just three years old, and Jolene's father, Pete — who's got terminal cancer and if she doesn't get to him quick … and *my wife, Thelma* — they're all going to die." The last words rode a sob out of his throat. He couldn't help it and he dropped his chin and looked at the floor.

"You can't do nothing even if I told you. They's too many of 'em."

"They?"

"They, it, the Jabberwock, don't matter what name you use, it's too big and mean and angry. It ain't gonna let them people go, no more'n it let my mama's people go. She begged and pleaded with it, but by then it was too late and they was all eat up to feed the dark, the black thing. It didn't take her, though. After what she done, it left her be."

"What did she do?"

Cotton held his breath. She said nothing, just looked at him.

Maybe her mind really was gone. Maybe she was refusing to tell him because she didn't remember what her mother'd said.

Perhaps she saw the skepticism on his face, because a crooked smile formed in the layers of wrinkles on her face.

"I remember it all, every detail" — she tapped an arthritis-gnarled finger on her temple — "in case you's worried I forgot." She let out a sigh. "All right, then. I'll tell you, but like I said, it ain't gonna do you no good to know."

Then she told him that her mother, a ten-year-old child, had scoured the forest floor for weeks, *months*, picking up the bones the miners had scattered there after the mining company man said they were the bones of the jitter dancers.

She told him what her mother had done with the bones.

Then she told him about her mother's confrontation with the Jabberwock.

"It was the terrible-est thing she ever did see," Rose said, and a shudder went through her frail old body. "Ever time she told me about it, and she told me about it over and over and … and ever time, she got scared again like it'd just happened.

. . .

IT TAKES LILY two trips to haul all the bones up to the spot on the mountainside where the miners had located the entrance to the burial cave where they'd found the bones. The opening wasn't very big, had been covered by a single large rock, but the miners had to dig through brush that had grown up around it. Wouldn't nobody have known the cave was there, covered up like it was, though once you found it, rolling the big rock away wasn't no problem because it was round. The bones had just been laid out on the floor, or that's what Lily had heard. Skeletons — some of them with ratty clothes still clinging to the bones. Little skeletons, which fell apart, of course, when the miners gathered up the bones and put them in duffle bags.

All that remains for Lily to do now is to put the bones back where they came from. Somebody'd buried them people in that cave and the miners had … what was it … a big word … desecrated. *Yes, they'd* desecrated *the grave by gathering all the bones up and hauling them down the mountain in duffle bags.*

Maybe if she does that, the Jabberwock won't be mad anymore — if that's what had made it mad in the first place. Maybe then the Jabberwock will let the people go. At least, that's what she'd thought when she first started gathering up the bones. But as time wore on, Lily came to believe there wasn't nobody left to release. She could sense deep inside her that everyone — her family and all the others, all the people in town, was dead.

Then collecting the bones became about Lily herself. She couldn't leave Gideon, had never ventured more than a mile away from her home in her whole life, had no idea what was out there beyond the mountains. Her only contact with that world had been with the mining company officials — evil men, all of them, who treated the miners like slaves. She would not go out into that world where she would be less than human. She would die if she ever left Gideon, wither up as surely as the blossom of a rose plucked from a bush.

But to stay here, she would have to make her peace with the

Jabberwock, or he'd eventually get around to taking her just like he had taken all the others. Doing right by the bones, puttin' 'em back in the grave, is the only way she can think to do that.

Once she has hauled both duffle bags full of bones up to the cave, she sits down on a rock next to the big one that'd been used to seal up the entrance, catching her breath.

She notices then how quiet it is. There are no birds singing in the trees, no cicadas in the bushes. The wind has stopped, and it begins to feel airless. She is frightened. But then, she has been frightened for so long she no longer really recalls what it feels like not to be afraid.

Afraid and alone.

It is getting late. She must get back to town, back to the safety of the houses before dark when the mists come, because it is in the mist that the haints cry out.

She picks up the smaller of the two duffle bags and steps toward the shadows of the entrance to the small cave. When she looks inside, she notices there are scratches all over the walls.

Suddenly, a voice cries out in the forest behind her. The voice isn't human, maybe once was but not anymore. The voice cries a word, a single anguished sound.

"No!"

Lily freezes, whirls around.

And there is a chorus of sounds from the nearby trees where a mist has gathered, voices, all them hideous and inhuman, all the more terrible by how almost-human they are.

No, don't.

Not there.

Don't put us back there!

Lily drops the duffle bag full of bones and starts to run back toward town, but the mist blocks her path, carrying with it voices, a dozen voices — more. All crying out in mournful misery.

She collapses to her knees, clamps her hands over her ears and sobs as shadows begin to swirl around her, faster and faster, their passage stirring up a wind that ruffles her hair.

She squeezes her eyes shut and begins to scream, to shriek, but the other voices are so loud she can't even hear her own.

Then it all stops. She keeps screaming but there is no other sound and her voice falters. Everything is quiet and still. Her hair settles back around her face when the wind dies. But it is only the movement that has stopped. The presence is still there. All around her. Waiting for her to open her eyes.

Finally she does, she sees them, what they are, and their voices speak to her without sound about hunger and terror and death. About clawing the walls trying to get out.

They are glad she has gathered them, brought them all back together, but she must not leave them here. They tell her where the bones must go, and she works with an energy she thought was totally spent to do as they direct.

She completes the task on her knees by the light of a full moon, her fingers raw from digging, bruised and scraped from making it fit. She will have to haul rocks from Troublesome Creek tomorrow to finish it, might take two days. But she has done what she was told to do and now she sits back and takes a deep, exhausted breath. Lily lifts her face toward the black velvet sky and the dark shadows that had swirled around her are there, part of the night now, and they no longer frighten her. She knows she has done them right. She knows that she can stay here, the Jabberwock will not harm her. No, more than that — she'll be protected.

The Jabberwock will take care of Lily Topple.

Cotton didn't even realize he had gotten to his feet and approached the old woman's bed as she told the tale, drawn there by the visions she painted in his head. Now, he stood beside Rose Topple, looking down at her. When her focus returned to the room, she looked up into his eyes.

"They was the horriblest creatures ever was on the earth, but my mama done right and they looked after her."

She shook her head. "They couldn't help what they was. It weren't their fault."

She paused, took a breath.

"Wasn't just them, neither. There was the … *other.* Mama didn't never see it, though. They kept her safe from it, kept it away."

Cotton didn't know what that meant, but he could see her focus fading and a not-there look begin to come into her eyes.

"So she 'done right by the Jabberwock' by gathering up the scattered bones, putting them together in one place — is that what you're saying?"

"She'd a'done more but she was just a little girl and couldn't do it proper. She done the best she could do."

And maybe that was the answer Cotton'd been looking for.

Chapter Thirty-Six

E.J. WAS SLEEPING. That was good. Even though Raylynn treasured every one of his awake and aware moments, counted them as prizes beyond value because they were finite and few, she was always grateful when he was asleep because when he was asleep he was not in pain. And no matter how much of a front he put up, she knew that he was always in agony when he was aware enough to know it.

Raylynn watched his chest move up and down. Up and down. And the sight was blurry because she was looking at it through the glaze of tears in her eyes that she only allowed when E.J. was asleep and she did not fear being disturbed by anybody. She held it together better if her shift was about to be up, if she was going to replaced by somebody long enough for her to do the absolute essentials — like run upstairs and get something to eat in E.J.'s apartment.

Malachi had actually moved into E.J.'s apartment, but was seldom there, just long enough to heat up a can of soup, catch a couple of hours of sleep, shave and take a shower. Raylynn lived on Pebble Bottom Road not far from the clinic, so sometimes she dashed home to change clothes, maybe even nap for a little while, but her understanding that E.J. had only hours left to live, and that she, too, was on the brink of eternity, made her reluctant to leave the clinic.

The Jabberwock had saved Raylynn. And it had sentenced E.J. to die. If there were no Jabberwock, E.J. could get the care he needed, he could receive the rabies shots that would make him desperately sick — but desperately sick was better than dead, was better than the slow death of rabies and that was how E.J. would die without the vaccine.

Except he wouldn't die that way. Raylynn had promised him she wouldn't let it happen. She had promised the man she loved that she would save him from dying the death of a mad dog, foaming at the mouth, snapping in vicious insanity at any live thing that came within his reach. She'd promised she'd steal enough Oxycontin to give E.J. so that he would not die a raging manic. He would merely go peacefully to sleep and never wake up.

She'd told him that, reassured him that she would save him from that fate. But she had *not* told him that she'd decided to join him in death, because there was no future for Raylynn without him. She had nothing to live for without E.J.

Raylynn Bennett had come to the end of the road. She would die if the Jabberwock remained. And she would die if it did not.

Even if the Jabberwock were somehow banished, defeated, or merely blew back out of the county with the same mystery with which it had blown in, Raylynn Bennett's life would be on a fatal countdown. In a post-Jabberwock world, her father would come home. He would walk back into the house — *his* house — and expect to take up with life just as he had left it.

And that *would not be.*

Her father would never touch her again.

Raylynn would kill him before he had a chance.

She even knew how, had worked it out in her head as she sat beside a sleeping E.J., watching the sheet on his chest rise and fall. She had replayed the fanciful scene in her head so often it was almost a reality.

Her father would come home. Would walk in the back door, calling for her. She would answer, as she always did, eyes averted because she didn't want to see the hunger in his eyes when he looked at her.

She would find a smile to paste on her lips, graciously put off all his questions — and surely he'd be curious about what had happened to Nowhere County! She'd offer to bring him a glass of iced tea, first. He loved super-sweet Southern iced tea, with lots of ice. She'd tell him to take his shoes off, sit back in his recliner and she'd bring it to him.

The glass would be laced with Oxycontin. Not enough to kill, just enough to render him unconscious. She wanted him awake and aware when she killed him. Then she would duct tape him to the chair, use a whole roll, around and around and around him from his chin to his ankles. When he came to, she would describe for him exactly how she planned to kill him.

She would hold out the ice pick, describe how she would stick it through his left eye, blinding him, but not killing him. Then she'd demonstrate! He would scream, wail, fight against the coming horror — just like she had wanted to do every time she heard him, *smelled* him come into her room at night. Then he would watch with his remaining eye as the ice pick came relentlessly toward him.

He'd beg, plead, cry maybe. Just like she had begged, pleaded and cried. And his terror would have no more effect on Raylynn than her terror had had on him. She would shove the icepick into his eye! Deeper. And deeper. And deeper. All the way up to the hilt in his eye socket. He would be dead. And she would be executed for premeditated murder.

Except she wouldn't. She and E.J. would exit this life on their own terms. E.J. wouldn't go mad. She wouldn't be executed. Neither of them would pass out of this world in the grip of some mindless monster as it absorbed them into itself.

She and E.J. would hold hands, look into each other's eyes and ...

"You asleep, too?"

Her head snapped up and she saw that E.J. was looking at her. He was awake and thought he had caught her dozing at his bedside. She hadn't been dozing, she was always totally awake and aware because the time with him was so precious and so limited.

She smiled at him.

"Wrongo, Moose Breath — that's what you and the others say, but I don't know what it means."

His smile was weak. His voice was airless.

"From an old television show," he gasped. She could see the agony in his eyes.

But it would be over soon.

"That's what Rocky the Flying Squirrel would say when Bullwinkle—"

"I have been stealing pills."

She heard herself say the words and wanted to call them back. She hadn't meant to blurt it out like that, had intended ...

Then she saw relief flood his face and she was glad

she'd told him, glad she had eased his mind even if it wasn't the way she'd intended.

"How did—?"

She put her finger to his lips.

"It doesn't matter how. I managed it, that's all that matters." She didn't want to alarm him, so she'd figured out how she would say what came next so as not to put him on alert.

"How many Oxycontin pills does it take for a fatal dose?" she asked.

"I don't know about the pills I'm taking — don't know the milligrams. But I'm sure ten or twelve of them taken at once … You have that many?"

She did have that many, but she did not yet have *twice* that many. She'd need another day for that.

"By tomorrow afternoon, I'll be ready. I can't take too many at one time or else Sam——"

"I understand. I … What's today? I am so drugged up, dopey and with all those nasties swimming around in my veins, I lose track of time."

"And time has already lost track of us." She had told him about the stars on only one side of the sky, and how too-fast time now seemed to be too-slow time. "But if the clocks and calendars are to be believed, it's Tuesday. And you have—"

"Seven days after infection … So we're good." He was breathing hard from the effort to speak. Still … she loved it when he went into "doctor" mode. He seemed almost like his old self then. "All the extrapolations of how long it takes for the virus to reach a sufficient level to cause symptoms … they're just educated guesses. Most certainly a little off and possibly a whole lot. Yeah, tomorrow. Wednesday. That's time. Wait as far as possible just in case … but not too long, not long enough for …"

"Yes. Tomorrow."

"Raylynn. I don't know how … what to—"

"Don't say anything — *please*! Just lie back and rest. Tomorrow—"

"Tomorrow," he said, dreamily.

"I'm going with you."

"What? What did you say?"

"I said I'm going with you. When you make your grand exit tomorrow … we'll go together. I'll have enough pills saved up for the two of us by then."

She was unprepared for the look of horror on his face.

"No! Raylynn, for God's sake, what are you talking about? No."

He was getting upset, moving around, which was banging his bandaged leg around. She knew the agony it caused him, watch his face twist in pain.

She felt around in the pocket of her smock and drew out a full bottle of pills, dropped two into her hand and held them out.

"I know it's early, but it doesn't matter now. I can tell it hurts. Take them."

"No, I'm not going to take anything to fuzzy my thinking because it's clear *you're* not thinking rationally. One of us has to. What do you mean 'we will go together'? That's crazy. Why would you—?"

"My father has been raping me since I was five years old."

She couldn't breathe. Where had those words come from? Never in her weakest moments did she even consider confessing to E.J. or anybody else what had been happening to her. She intended to take those nightmare images with her to the grave.

"I am so sorry … I didn't mean to say that. It's just—"

"He will *never* touch you again. *I promise you.* Never! But you don't have to die to escape him."

"I'm not just dying to run away from him. I am dying so I can leave the world with you. I don't want to live in a world without you, E.J. I … I love you."

He just looked at her. Then he began to cry. He cried softly, weakly until he went back to sleep.

Chapter Thirty-Seven

TIME TELESCOPED. Part of the reason was exhaustion, of course. Sam didn't sleep last night, sitting up with Rusty. But it was also the intensity of the situation that did screwy things with Sam's mind. Everything in life had been intense since J-Day, and Sam couldn't let her mind wander back down the paths of all the horror she'd had to deal with since then. If she did, she would get lost in it and never find her way back.

She had done everything she could with Essie's wound. She'd removed the bloody tee shirt, cleaned the area and put a sterile pressure bandage in its place.

The wound itself was small, no bigger than the end of Sam's thumb. Whoever had shot her had used a small-caliber gun to do it, and you'd think in a drive-by, a shooter would be wielding some big rifle. But she didn't let her mind go there, either because she couldn't wrap her mind around how life had come to the point that a nowhere person would drive down Main Street in Persimmon Ridge and shoot a poor handicapped girl sitting on a porch.

It had been about Viola, of course. A warning of some

kind? Revenge for something she'd done, and Lord knows the line of people who could lay claim to that motive would stretch out so far you couldn't see the end.

The blood was still flowing, but not in the amounts that had soaked the tee shirt. Even if the new pressure bandage stopped the bleeding entirely, it wouldn't save her life. Essie was still bleeding internally, from puncture wounds in her colon, and those wounds were oozing into her abdominal cavity, slowly filling it with blood and fecal material that would poison her whole system.

And Sam couldn't do a thing about it.

She didn't try to move Essie off the examining room table because there was no other room to put her in, and no Malachi handy to go somewhere and fetch her a bed.

Malachi.

Where was Malachi?

He'd left to pick up Rev. Norman at nine o'clock this morning. Sam had moved on from curious and mildly annoyed to genuine concern. Something had happened, and if her own experience since J-Day was any indication, that something was bad.

All the somethings were bad.

Sam left the room only once and went down the hallway to check on the other two patients. Rusty lay as if sleeping on the bed Malachi had "borrowed" from Martha Whittiker's house. She had to keep herself from reaching out and shaking him, telling him to wake up and get dressed or he'd be late for school.

Judd Perkins sat with the boy, a big bear of a man on a small chair, looking a little like an elephant sitting on a football.

"He's gonna wake up," Judd told her quietly. "I know you're scared to death right now, but it's gonna be fine. I b'lieve that. I really do."

She was sure he really did believe it. But that didn't make it true.

She stuck her head into E.J.'s room. He was sleeping, too, with Raylynn resolutely at his side. She'd sensed a change in Raylynn in the last day or two. She seemed calmer. More … something like "serene." She had been so terribly worried about E.J. that she'd been half out of her mind. But then, she'd chilled out. She was as attentive as always, maybe more so, wanted to spend every possible second she could with him, but she didn't appear to be frantic with worry anymore.

Maybe she was just too tired to be frantic. The level of exhaustion in everyone Sam knew — walking around on only a few hours of sleep at night, and one horror crisis after another every day — must be like fighting a war. Malachi would relate to that.

Malachi. Where was Malachi?

She passed by the waiting room on her way back down the hallway to Essie's room. Viola had parked all three of her sons there. Neb had on a tee-shirt that was several sizes too big for him and that was saying a lot. She couldn't imagine where he'd gotten it — perhaps the Dollar General Store, though there was almost nothing left in the building. Not many of the people who'd looted the place, who'd just taken whatever they needed, could wear a shirt that big so maybe that's why it'd been left behind. Neb sat off by himself, away from the other two, his eyes downcast, looking sightlessly at the floor. Zach and Obie sat side by side, talking quietly. They looked up at her, something like hope in her eyes, when she passed by the waiting room, but she just averted her eyes. Surely, Viola'd made it clear to them that there was nothing to hope for.

The sound of something like singing came from the

exam room where Essie lay, and Sam paused at the door, listening before she went inside.

"Ahhh-nah, gahma-gahma-gahma, so-so-wissy-wheeee."

The voice was Viola's. The words were nonsense, not sung, really, but chanted in a kind of rhythm that resembled a melody.

Sam opened the door and quietly stepped inside. Viola was holding her daughter's hand, had leaned over the girl's body so her face was close to Essie's and was chanting the words softly.

"Gonna be jest fine, baby girl, ain't nothing gonna hurt you, I won't let it. Ahhh-nah, gahma-gahma-gahma, so-so-wissy-wheeee. And soon's you're feeling better, I'm gonna take you on back home. You don't like the new house, so we ain't gonna stay there. You can go back to your own room, sleep in your own bed. Shhhhh. Shhhh, now. Gahma-gahma-gahma, so-so-wissy."

Sam approached the table and could see that the girl's breath had become shallow and ragged, each intake shaky, each exhale a trembling sigh.

Viola looked up at Sam.

"Go get the boys. They need to be here."

Sam turned and went out to the waiting room and returned with the three Tackett boys. They were grown men, of course, but Sam and everybody else saw them as "the Tackett boys."

The exam room was small, and with all the Tacketts there it felt airless. Sam remained by the door as Viola crooked her finger at first one and then the other of her sons.

"Kiss yore sister," she told Obie, and he obediently leaned over and kissed her cheek, then stepped away as Zach moved toward the bed. He held out a ratty Barbie doll with scraggly blonde hair. There was something sticky in the doll's hair. Maybe it was blood.

"I knowed you'd want this." Essie's eyes were unfocused, open but seeing nothing. When she didn't take the doll, Zach put it down on the table beside her. "Didn't take me no time at all to go into the Ridge and fetch it back here."

Viola frowned at him for that, then said to Essie, "'Member when I got you your Barbie … 'member that? It was that Christmas when it snowed so deep we couldn't hardly get the front door open. You was so happy. You 'member?"

Viola fit the doll into Essie's limp fingers.

Neb hung back. When Viola motioned him forward he just stood, shook his head. Tears were running down his cheeks.

Before Viola had a chance to summon him a second time, Essie made a gurgling sound in her throat, like she was choking.

"Now, it's okay, don't you never mind nothing," Viola crooned, "just breathe easy and you gonna be fine, shhh, shhh now, ahhh-nah, gahma-gahma-gahma, so-so-wissy-wheeee. Shhh."

Essie let out the breath she'd struggled to draw in and then lay still. The room was silent, no sound of her labored breathing.

Viola let out a sound then, more like a grunt than a cry, and leaned over and put her cheek against her daughter's.

No one moved. The only sound was Viola's voice, humming the not-melody of the nonsense song.

Then the door behind them opened and Malachi stepped into the room.

Sam sucked in a breath when she saw him, but made no sound. He was banged up and scraped up, scratched all over. Looked like he'd been dragged behind a car. There was dried blood on his forehead and down his cheek from a wound where blood had matted his black hair. His hands — fingers were raw, scuffed knuckles bleeding. His left forearm, wrist and the top of his hand were abraded like a kid's knee when he dumps his bike in the street.

"Mama?" he asked, clearly unaware of what had happened.

"She's gone," Viola said simply, her voice tear-clotted.

Malachi crossed the room in two long strides and took Essie's limp hand, looking in confusion at his mother.

"She was shot," Viola said. And the timber of her voice then was not anguish, the pain of loss or grief. It was barely harnessed rage. "Shot in the belly and she bled to death."

"Who …?"

"I do not know the answer to that question, son," she said, her words measured. "But I will find out. As God is my witness, I will find out."

Chapter Thirty-Eight

COTTON DIDN'T GO DIRECTLY BACK HOME after his conversation with Rose Topple. He made several important stops in Beaufort County first. Neither Jolene nor Stuart spoke when he was finished telling the story that had been told to him by the old woman in the Carlisle nursing home. The three looked from one to the other, sharing their disbelief and shock with their eyes.

Finally, Jolene found her voice.

"No wonder those spirits ..." She had to grab another breath to continue. "No wonder they were so disturbed, so agitated."

"You think that's it, then," Stuart said, his eyes bloodshot, his face haggard. "The bones. The little girl made peace with the Jabberwock when she gathered them up ..."

"... so maybe we can make peace with it if we do what she couldn't do," Cotton said.

He had thought about it all the way home, and even though his brain was foggy from lack of sleep, it still seemed like the only avenue open to them.

"And that is?" Jolene said.

"We bury the bones. Put them in a proper grave, have a service, put up a marker, *respect* those poor souls."

"It's not just them, though, is it?" Jolene said. "The unburied ones. There's something else. Something more."

"Something worse," Stuart said.

"Yes, I believe there is, but we can only do what we can do. I went to Home Depot and got the tools we'll need for the job." But that's not all Cotton got while he was in Carlisle. He'd stopped by a friend's house and borrowed another "tool" he prayed they wouldn't have to use. Tomorrow, we'll go to Fearsome Hollow and get the bones …"

"If they're still where she put them," Jolene said.

"Right. *If.* It's been almost a hundred years. In a century …" Stuart said.

"Like I said, we can only do what we can do."

They fell silent again then. Each a prisoner of their own hopes and fears. And the specter of night was on them. It would be dark soon and they must not sleep or the nightmare monsters will come for them. How could they possibly function tomorrow if they stayed up another night?

Cotton shook his head. One step at a time. He was too exhausted, his thinking too muddied to venture out there into tomorrow. He could only do the next thing, the step in front of him.

"Enough about tomorrow — only have a handful of synapses still firing and if I'm not careful they'll set my hair on fire. Tell me what the two of you did today."

"We did what *we* could do," Jolene said. "We went to my father's house and took the map off the wall, took it to Persimmon Ridge and put it up in the West Liberty Middle School auditorium, smack in the middle of the big wall in the back. We used stickpins to spell out a message. Couldn't say much, so pretty basic: 'Looking for you. Reply.' But we used three stickpins for each letter so you can't miss them."

"I'm not hopeful it will do any good," Stuart said. "Your father figured out the message because he was familiar with the map, saw that the stickpins had been moved. Just some random person looking at it ..."

"And the blackboard?" Cotton asked.

"Took it off the wall in Charlie's mother's house and took it to the veterinary clinic," Jolene said.

"Where'd you put it?"

"On the wall in the waiting room, above a row of chairs."

"What did you say?"

"As much as we could fit on there. It wasn't a very big chalkboard."

"I was careful to leave the note about birdseed, though," Stuart said. "Charlie's mother must have written it and maybe Charlie never erased it because it was ... you know, a message from her mother. Charlie would think something like that. I wrote as much as I could fit there. Charlie will recognize my handwriting — she'll know I wrote it."

"We told them who we are, that we're looking for them," Jolene said, "that as far as we can see, everybody in Nowhere County has vanished."

"And about the Jabberwock, how it wipes out memories, and what happened to us in Fearsome Hollow."

"We asked who was there ... on the other end," Jolene said. Cotton knew they were seeking names — that Pete, Charlie, Merrie and Thelma were still alive. "Told them about the suddenly-old houses."

"Did you tell them about Reece and—?"

"No!" Then Stuart said, more softly, "We don't really even know what happened there so what's the point in telling them about it? We did say you'd gone to talk to Rose Topple. And we said to erase what we'd written and write something in its place, tell us what happened to them. Just that much filled the whole blackboard."

"If that veterinary clinic has become the only medical facility in town, *someone* will see it eventually," Jolene said.

"If they can see what we've put there from wherever they are," Stuart said.

"We'll go back in the morning and see what they replied," Jolene said.

"*If* they replied," Cotton said.

"We need to tell them what Rose Topple said about the bones her mother hid, that we're going to—" Stuart said.

"We can do that on our way to Fearsome Hollow in the morning. By then, we'll know if we're getting through," Cotton said.

"You sound like you don't think we will," Jolene said.

"The only time we 'made contact' was in the presence of the Jabberwock. When it was in your father's house the day we had the freak show, and when you sensed the opposition in Charlie's mother's house. The Jabberwock was there then … and later, when it wasn't there …"

"Nothing," Stuart said. "Just empty buildings."

"But it wasn't just the presence of the Jabberwock," Jolene said. "It was the presence of people. Somebody was *there* … on the other side. Somebody responded by adding pins to the map, and Charlie wrote a message back to you." She looked at Stuart. "When we went back after we picked up the equipment at Reece Tibbits's house, maybe my father and Charlie … just weren't home at the time."

"Maybe it requires *both* — the presence of other people *and* the Jabberwock," Stuart said.

"And maybe it requires *only one* — *either* the Jabberwock *or* other people," Jolene said doggedly. "If that's the case, perhaps we're onto something."

"We've done all we can," Cotton said. "If we can make contact, we'll tell them what we're about to do."

The three fell silent, then Stuart said softly, "There's a lot riding on that little chalkboard message."

Chapter Thirty-Nine

Merrie burst into the breakroom calling out, "Mommy, come see. Come see what I finded in the waitin' woom."

Charlie was distracted. "I'll come in a minute. Mommy's busy right now."

It was late. The sun had not yet set out there on the flat, but shadowed twilight oozed out from beneath the trees in the hollows of Nowhere County. The Breakfast Club sat together, sipping bad coffee. It was the first chance they'd had to share more than bits and snatches of what'd happened to them that day.

Charlie had arrived at the clinic while Sam was looking after Essie Tackett, and had kept herself and Merrie judiciously out of sight. She'd stepped out into the hallway when she heard Malachi had returned, however, and ran into Viola, who hadn't been so distraught with grief that she failed to shoot Charlie a menacing look. Then Viola drove away with her daughter's body, and Sam shooed Malachi back into the clinic to clean up his wounds.

That he'd gotten when *Duncan Norman had tried to kill him.*

Charlie's head was swimming. Like she and the others were circling the drain of some horrible outcome, and the monstrousness and horror grew with every revolution as they got closer and closer to the black nothingness that threatened to swallow them all whole.

How many dead now?

Charlie shook her head, had literally lost count.

Add two more. Poor handicapped Esther Ruth Tackett and the Rev. Duncan Norman. There was no sense searching for his body in the dark, but Malachi would deal with that as soon as it got light tomorrow. Charlie had seen the look of profound gratitude wash over Sam's face when Pete Rutherford offered to carry the news about the minister's death to his wife, Miriam.

First her daughter. Then her husband.

On and on and on.

Charlie wanted to curse and scream and … just sit in a corner somewhere and sob. Instead, she tried to concentrate on making sure she didn't leave out something important in her description of her encounter with Fish.

"He said it, the Jabberwock *killed* that guy?" Sam was still having trouble getting her arms around that part. "It was a thing, a real *thing* — not … just some apparition in the mist?"

"It was a real thing when it picked up our car the day we went to Fearsome Hollow with the Tungates looking for Abner," Malachi said.

Charlie felt so sorry for Malachi. Oh, not because he was bunged up — and he was, scratched and scraped and bleeding all over, most certainly had at least a mild concussion. But she figured he'd probably seen worse on a bad day in boot camp. It was the emotional wounds you couldn't see that she knew hurt a lot worse than clocking his head on a rock. His sister was dead, had been shot by

… who knew? He'd walked in seconds too late to tell her goodbye, and his mother'd been as cold as wind off a glacier. Sam said Viola'd told Malachi she didn't need him, or his brothers, for that matter, to "see to Essie." Said that was woman's work, and she'd call Malachi about "the service" tomorrow.

Not that Charlie claimed to be great at reading people, but it'd be safe money to bet Viola Tackett was way more angry over her daughter's death than she was grief-stricken. Somebody had *shot her daughter,* and Viola would look under every rock and down every rabbit hole in the county to find out who it was. Charlie would *not* want to be that person when Viola caught up with them!

"Even that day, all we could *see* were shapes in the mist — certainly not a creature with teeth and claws," Charlie said. "You should have seen the scars on Fish's chest!" She shuddered. "No wonder he crawled into a bottle afterward and never came out. What he described was a right-off-a-movie-set monster. Correction: monster**s**. Plural. More than one."

"The more-than-one-part fits," Sam said. "We heard whispers in the mist that day when we were first-graders." She looked at Malachi. "You said you thought it was the other children at the fair. And what Abby said — everything fits that the Jabberwock is a 'them.'"

"Mommeeee," Merrie wailed. "I finded it on da wall and it wasn't dere before — you have to come see *now!*"

"Remember what we talked about — how whining isn't allowed."

"But I did ask in my sweet voice," Merrie countered. "You didn't come, so din I whined."

Charlie caught a small smile on Malachi's face.

"What?"

"Well, she did ask in a sweet voice …" he said.

"It's a blackboard. Come on, I show you."

"Is there a blackboard somewhere …?"

Sam shook her head.

Charlie got up and allowed Merrie to drag her out of the room toward the clinic waiting room.

"One of da puppies — the black one wiff one white ear. He gotted out of the pen and I had to chased him. That's when I see-ed it."

Merrie let go of her mother's hand and raced ahead of her. When Charlie saw what was affixed to the far wall above the chairs in the waiting room, her knees felt like bags of water. She walked as if in a trance to stand in front of the blackboard that had been nailed there.

Printed on the top of the blackboard were the words: "Not in Kansas Anymore, *TO-DO*"

How did …?

Who …?

She gulped in enough air not to pass out and found her voice, told Merrie to go get Sam and Malachi, tell them her mother needed them *right now.*

When the others arrived, they stood staring in disbelief at the blackboard that had not been there the last time they were in the clinic waiting room.

"Where'd that come from?" Sam asked.

"Wait a minute — isn't that the—?" Malachi began, then Charlie finally found enough air to speak.

"It's not just some random blackboard … it's the one from my mother's kitchen."

That was a conversation stopper.

"The one where the words appeared in your husband's handwriting?" Sam asked, but it wasn't a question.

"And where the Jabberwock wrote 'Stay and play with me,'" Malachi said, not a question either.

They had planned on trying to use the blackboard to

communicate with the Jabberwock, see if they could talk to it as it had talked to Charlie. But the plan was interrupted by a trial … a dead teenager … and Toby … then Hayley's body and Rusty … It just went on and on and—

"Who brought it here?" Sam asked. "Went to your mother's house, took it down, and nailed it to the wall here?"

Charlie found she only had the energy to shake her head and shrug.

"And for what purpose?" Malachi followed.

Sam and Malachi took the ball and ran with it — coming up with first one explanation and then another about how the blackboard had ended up in the veterinary clinic waiting room, who had moved it, and why.

Merrie tugged on Charlie's hand and pointed proudly to the big round thing in the center of the blackboard. "I drawed it for you, Mommy. It's a flower, but wiff just white chalk, no pretty colors."

The drawing could have been a flower on a stem and lots of leaves. It could also have been a dead spider. Or a splatter of white paint. The little girl had had to climb up onto the seat of a chair to reach the blackboard on the wall. There was chalk dust sifted like powdered sugar on the chair cushion outlining two little footprints. It was only then that Charlie noticed the top of Merrie's sneakers.

"How'd you get that chalk all over your shoes?" she asked.

Merrie picked up the eraser resting beside a piece of chalk in the metal tray attached to the blackboard. "It comed off dis when I used it."

Then Charlie noticed that the *only* thing on the blackboard was the big flower and its associated appendages. *Nothing else.*

She had trouble finding the air to speak.

"Did you … *erase* …?"

"Uh huh. I had to wiped it all off, 'rased it clean so I could make da flower big as the sky."

When the blackboard had hung in her mother's kitchen, there had been nothing on it — *except* the words "get bird seed" in her mother's handwriting. *Her mother's words!* Charlie had been so careful to leave them. They'd been all she had, the last words her mother … Now, they were gone.

Charlie was surprised at the surge of emotion that welled up in her chest — so fierce it even muted the shock of finding the blackboard here. Tears filled her eyes and spilled down her cheeks.

The little girl hadn't known what she was doing, didn't realize when she erased the blackboard that she was destroying something of incalculable importance. Merrie didn't know she was wiping away words written in the handwriting of someone Charlie loved desperately.

Now, the message that had been on the blackboard was lost forever.

Chapter Forty

THE BOYS BROUGHT Essie's dead body home to the Nower — to the *Tackett* House — in the back of Obie's black pickup truck, carried her upstairs to the big bathroom off Viola's bedroom and lay her on the floor where Viola could see to her. Then she made them all leave.

"Shoo outta here, git!" she told Obie, Zach and Neb. "This here is private female stuff."

She didn't have to send Malachi away. She'd done that already. Oh, not because she was mad at him, though she was. She didn't have all the puzzle pieces yet, but she knew what he'd done. Not exactly the how, when and where of it, but she knew enough. He'd killed Howie Witherspoon, and might even have been in self-defense. Malachi coulda gone over there to threaten him, warn him not to hurt that boy Toby Malachi was so determined to protect. Maybe Howie'd drawn down on him and Malachi didn't have no choice. It really didn't matter anymore to Viola.

Funny how things changed up inside you like that, how something that'd seemed so important suddenly wasn't important at all. And what hadn't never mattered a fig to you was about the onliest thing in the world that did.

She'd told Malachi to stay where he was at, that she didn't want the help of none of her boys. She needed to see to their sister private-like. Then she'd asked real nice, well, as nice as she was able, for him to come on over tomorrow about noon. She'd have Essie all laid out proper and the whole family needed to gather round and do the funeral and the burying.

He'd asked her about that part, but she'd put him off, said she needed time to think on it and figure out what exactly it was she wanted to do. Which wasn't true, of course. Viola already knew what she was gonna do — about the burial, anyway, had figured that part out the same way she'd decided to take the Nower House to live in. They was things in life she and her kin had been denied that other people had, and now it was time to collect on all that had been kept from them. They would live like they wanted, where they wanted, do whatever they wanted with whomever — whatever suited them. Shoot, she'd been planning that part as she'd bumped along in the truck back to the day she'd rode the Jabberwock. She seen the opportunity then, and set out to lay her plans. And she'd accomplished everything she had set out to do, just like she'd plotted it out.

But they was things that come up she hadn't planned for, couldn't a'planned for. That Charlie woman, the loudmouth who was gonna be payback to her youngest son for his bad judgement in doing what his mama'd said he couldn't do.

Then this morning she'd found out … stumbled upon … wouldn't never in the world have dreamed possible. As she'd sat in the kitchen in the old house in Turkey Neck

Hollow looking at that snapshot of Malachi, the world had sorta shifted under her. Like that kaleidoscope thing that rested on that little gold pedestal in the "library" of the Tackett House. Obie'd about made his self go blind looking into it. Viola thought it was right pretty her own self, though it made her uneasy the way you could look at the colored rocks through that little tube and a bunch of mirrors and all you had to do was turn it and the same rocks would look entirely different.

The world had seemed to do a kaleidoscope thing on her earlier today. She'd made Zach drive slow back into town, that picture snug in the pocket of her dress, even though he wanted to zoom fast as he could in that fancy sports car. And she'd thought about the only one of her kids that had ever been worthy of drawing life from her body. Malachi. Tall, strong, handsome, smart Malachi.

Malachi who had gone his own way his whole life, hadn't never been the obedient boy she'd wanted him to be. Malachi, who'd been lost to her when he come home so damaged from the war ... and then soon's he started to come out of it, he had walked away his own self to take up with them as opposed to her.

Malachi, the last and best of her git.

Only, maybe now he wasn't that after all. Maybe they was another of her seed, a second chance for her to have the boy she deserved as her son and heir.

All that had been spinning around in her mind when Zach pulled that fancy car to a screeching stop in the driveway of the Tackett House and she seen Neb waddling toward the backyard, carrying Essie in his arms.

And what he told her had burned every other thought out of her head.

Somebody had shot Essie. Shot her!

Viola'd put away the rage at such a blasphemy — an innocent like poor fat Essie who wouldn't hurt nobody being gunned down — but she'd put that anger away so's she could care for her daughter. She'd known soon's she saw her that she was kilt. They was too much blood and shot in the belly like she was. But Viola done everything she could do to save the girl's life, took her to the only help they was. And then she'd sat with her, was a good mama to her, eased the poor little thing outta this life and into the next one.

Viola still had obligations, kinship obligations. She had to do right by her girl, lay her to rest proper. But not up there in the mountains around Killarney, out there in the cemetery with all them little crosses marking the graves of the others of her children who didn't even live long enough for her to get to know who they was, what they was like. Essie wasn't going to join her brothers and sisters in the family cemetery. That was a place where poor people buried their dead and Viola Tackett wasn't a poor person anymore. She'd put her Essie in a place that befitted a member of the Tackett family. She had already decided where that would be.

That left only getting Essie ready.

She washed her, got her clean, using a sponge and that sweet-smelling soap that was in all the bathrooms in the house. Might be that Essie was cleaner and smelled better dead than she ever had alive. She woulda liked to wash Essie's hair, but wasn't no way to do that, there being so much of it. But Viola brushed it until she got out every snarl and tangle, then she braided it in them fat braids that hung down over her shoulders.

Essie didn't have no nice clothes. Didn't even own a dress, hadn't owned one since she was a little girl. She wore them overalls that was easy for her to get into and out of, and tee shirts, and sometimes a baggy sweatshirt in the wintertime, though she never did seem to get too hot nor too cold. She was fine whatever the temperature.

Viola had been gonna wash up the clothes of everybody in the family, in that washing machine down in the basement, dry them in the dryer with them little sheets of good-smelling stuff that was supposed to make them soft. But she hadn't got 'round to all that yet, and Essie didn't have nothing that was clean. So she done all she could do, and it was just fine. She took that pretty lace bedspread off'n Essie's bed and wrapped her up in it, pinned it around her so's it almost looked like a dress — a pretty white wedding dress for a girl wouldn't never have got married. It was fitting she should go to her grave like that.

She'd made the boys stay out of her way downstairs, didn't even holler to get somebody to come up and help her drag Essie into the bedroom, where she laid out a pretty quilt that'd been on the bed in the room that was now Obie's. She dragged Essie onto it and folded it around her. They'd take her out tomorrow like that, carry her in that quilt to her final resting place. She'd send Obie and Neb in the morning to make everything ready.

Viola looked down at her daughter. Her face wasn't no more expressionless in death than it'd been most of the time in life.

And finally … finally, Viola let go of her hold on her rage.

She'd kept it in check, kept hold of it because they was more important things to do, things it was her responsibility to get done and done right. Well, she'd done them.

Now, she sat down on the bed and allowed rage to flow over her in wave after fiery wave. She hadn't never been mad as she was at that moment. Not one time in her near seven decades of drawing breath, had not ever ached to hurt someone the way she ached to hurt the person who had put a bullet in her poor Essie.

And Viola would do that. She would make them pay. She would spend every last ounce of the strength she possessed on this earth to find who had shot her baby girl and hurt them. Mess them up good!

She'd already set the ball rolling, had got Zach to call that phone tree thing right after they got Essie to the clinic, so wouldn't be nobody in the county who didn't know about the "county meeting."

She'd made sure everybody would show up by promising the one thing that'd bring 'em all running. *Gasoline.* She'd instructed Zack to say that all the stories they'd been hearing was true — Viola Tackett had an inexhaustible supply. And she was going to give it out *free* to anybody who needed some. All they had to do was come to the meeting and put they names on a list. She'd send Zack zipping around the county all morning in his fancy car and Obie in his black pickup, stopping and showing folks their full tanks of gas!

She would gather the whole lot of them on Main Street in front of the school, packed tight, stretched out up and down the street in both directions. Then Viola would tell them the real truth, that they'd been summoned to cough up the person who had murdered her daughter. She'd have her boys and whoever else she could round up stationed all around, armed to catch any runners.

Viola could see in her mind's eye what she would do. She'd grab the person closest to her, just grab anybody random-like, and she'd put a gun to their head and announce.

"I'm going to count to three, and if don't nobody tell me who killed my daughter, I'm going to pull the trigger.

And I am going to keep shooting people, one after another, until somebody tells me the truth. If I have to shoot every man, woman and child in Nowhere County to get to the person I'm looking for … well, bullets is cheap."

THE END

The adventures of the residents of Nower County (aka Nowhere), USA, continue in *Nowhere People*, Nowhere, USA Book 7.

Get Nowhere People today!

A Note from the Author

Thank you for reading *Blown Away*.

If you enjoyed this book, you please consider writing a review on your favorite bookselling site so other readers might enjoy it too. Just a couple of sentences would mean a lot to me.

Thank you!

Ninie Hammon

About the Author

Ninie Hammon (rhymes with shiny, not skinny) grew up in Muleshoe, Texas, got a BA in English and theatre from Texas Tech University and snagged a job as a newspaper reporter. She didn't know a thing about journalism, but her editor said if she could write he could teach her the rest of it and if she couldn't write the rest of it didn't matter. She hung in there for a 25-year career as a journalist. As soon as she figured out that making up the facts was a whole lot more fun than reporting them, she turned to fiction and never looked back.

Ninie now writes suspense--every flavor except pistachio: psychological suspense, inspirational suspense, suspense thrillers, paranormal suspense, suspense mysteries.

In every book she keeps this promise to her Loyal Reader: "I will tell you a story in a distinctive voice you'll always recognize, about people as ordinary as you are--people who have been slammed by something they didn't sign on for, and now they must fight for their lives. Then smack in the middle of their everyday worlds, those people encounter the unexplainable--and it's always the game-changer."

Also By Ninie Hammon

Cornbread Mafia

Fire In The Hole

Blown' Up A Storm

Ridin' For A Fall

Nowhere, USA

The Jabberwock

Mad Dog

Trapped

The Hanging Judge

The Witch of Gideon

Blown Away

Nowhere People

Through The Canvas Series

Black Water

Red Web

Gold Promise

Blue Tears

The Taken Saga

The Taken

The Changed

The Hidden

The Saved

The Unexplainable Collection

Five Days in May

Black Sunshine

The Based on True Stories Collection

Home Grown

Sudan

When Butterflies Cry

The Knowing Series

The Knowing

The Deceiving

The Reckoning

The Fault

Stand-alone Psychological Thrillers

The Memory Closet

The Last Safe Place